BREEDER

BREEDER

HONNI VAN RIJSWIJK

BLACK STONE PUBLISHING

Printed in the United States of America

First edition: 2021
ISBN 978-1-0940-9980-4
Young Adult Fiction / Science Fiction / General

1 3 5 7 9 10 8 6 4 2

CIP data for this book is available
from the Library of Congress

Blackstone Publishing
31 Mistletoe Rd.
Ashland, OR 97520

www.BlackstonePublishing.com

For Laura and Anika,
Mum and Dad,
Chris and Matt and Ness,
Pat and Jenny,
Beth,
Jo and Rachael and Sophie,
with all my love.

BREEDER

My name is Will. Naming me was the last thing my mother did before she died. Sometimes I tell myself a story for comfort. In this story, my mother wanted to give me a name that was a secret message, the only one she would get through to me. I imagine that my mother looked back over her short and crappy life and thought about all the hell that lay ahead for me, and the message she wanted to pass on was *Have strength, be resilient. Will. I give you Will.* Sometimes I even imagine that she wanted to say something more—*I'm happy you were born, Will. I love you and want you to survive.* But I don't think she actually loved me, and I know she wasn't happy that I was born. She killed herself a couple of hours after I came into this world. I don't blame her—she was only thirteen years old.

The note she left behind just said: "Baby Name Will." She couldn't write that well—she was a Breeder, after all, so she'd never been to school. My ma never, ever talks about her, or about what happened, and mostly, I don't dare ask.

My name Is Will. I'm u Westie. I live in Zone F. My Corporation account is in credit. These are the things I say clearly and quickly to any CSO—Corporation Security Officer—who asks. These are the facts that flash on a screen whenever I push my wrist against a security scanner: when I get on the bus, when I log on at school or work, and when I go through my front door in the evening. Twenty times a day—at least.

"Will?"

I look up. Sir is frowning at me. "We're waiting," he says. I nod, staring at the icons on my screen. I'm nauseated—everyone is. It's Evaluation Day. But for me, it's also because of the Crystal 8 withdrawals.

I click on the first icon, profile, and everyone watches my screen projection at the front of the classroom.

NAME: Meadows, Will
SEX: Male
TYPE: Westie
AGE: 15

GUARDIAN: Meadows, Jessica
SIBLINGS: 0
ACADEMICS: Average
PHYSICAL: Below Average
PSYCHOLOGY: Average
EMPLOYMENT: Desalination Plant—Technical
LONG-TERM TRACK: Desalination Plant—Technical

"Next screen, please, Will," Sir says. He's alright, Sir: he suffers almost as much as we do each Evaluation Day, and you can feel him wishing us all to pass. Not like our teacher last year—that bastard looked ecstatic whenever there was a Corp alert, and he *loved* it when Craig Jacobsen's screen flashed UNSATISFACTORY and we went into lockdown until the CSOs arrived and took Craig to the Rator. They didn't even send Craig to the Circle for retraining—just straight to the fucking Rator.

The tension rises as I hover over the second icon: UNITS. Our units are aggregated daily and reported every month on Evaluation Day. But the Corp changes the algorithm each month, so you can never tell for certain whether you're going to measure up.

"Will?" Sir says again; his tone is anxious.

I click, and quickly scan to the bottom of the screen.

UNITS INVESTED IN WILL MEADOWS
BY THE CORPORATION TO DATE:
- SOCIAL: 42,687
- MATERIAL: 54,679
- EDUCATION: 19,677

UNITS RETURNED TO THE CORPORATION
BY WILL MEADOWS TO DATE:
- **WORK OUTPUT: 33,543**
- **EDUCATION OUTPUT: 0 (N/A—Westie, Zone F)**
- **GENETIC OUTPUT: 0 (N/A—Westie, Zone F)**
- **PROJECTED GENETIC OUTPUT: 0 (N/A—Westie, Zone F)**
- **PROJECTED LIFETIME DEBT OWED TO THE CORPORATION: 480,000**
- **PROJECTED RATE OF PAY-OFF: 12,000/year**
- **PROJECTED TIME TO PAY OFF: 40 years**
- **PROJECTED RATE OF PAY-OFF: Satisfactory**

OVERALL RESULT: SATISFACTORY

Satisfactory. Everyone claps. My mind buzzes as Sir smiles at me and then moves on to Sandeep Michaels. I breathe out, relieved. I wasn't really *that* worried, since each month I hustle extra units on the side through the Gray Corps. Hustling Gray units isn't a problem—as Ma says, the Corp usually looks the other way at the Gray economy, because the Corp benefits from it. But you never know if someone has been secretly reporting on you for working too slowly during a shift or cracking a joke about the Corp to the wrong person, which is what happened to Craig.

As Westies, we are allowed to be in a state of increasing debt to the Corp until we turn twelve—then we're expected to return units. Our class started out with half days at the desalination plant and now we all do four and a half days per week. Our half day of "school" is timetabled for different days each week—it depends on when we're most needed at the plant. On high-demand weeks, they just skip timetabling our school session altogether, which is fine with me. It's not like we're actually getting an education. All we do is go through our history and discuss ways to maximize the units we can give back to our generous Corporation, which has so selflessly protected us.

We've been evaluated every month since we were toddlers. If you're a Westie male, you get sent to a training center as soon as you're toilet trained. The center matches you to a school and future workplace, based on your zone and test metrics, as well as any units your family is able to give you. If you're very lucky, your parents and grandparents have earned a lot of Legacy units from the Corp to pass down to you. If that happens, you may get sent to a proper school in Zone E; we sure don't have any in Zone F.

For Zone F Westie guys like me, with zero Legacy units, there's nowhere to go. I'm of average intelligence and slightly below average in physical health. If I'm lucky, and I work hard and keep up my side hustles, I'll get to keep working at the desal plant. Hopefully, in twenty years or so, I'll have saved up enough units to buy a Shadow from the Incubator. Maybe she and I will be one of the 5 percent who have live births, and we'll work our asses off to give a surplus of units to our son. Maybe I could give that kid a chance at a Zone E life in plant management, or even, dare to dream, a semiprofessional job in Zone D.

If I'm unlucky, I'll screw up my units and get sent to the Rator.

For Breeders, of course, things are much worse. They're born into debt that they're not allowed to pay off themselves. But that's another story.

After evaluation, it's time for history. Sir puts on *The Horrors of the End Times*. All our history lessons are based on this two-hour Corp documentary, and we've watched it about six hundred times. The documentary stars and is narrated by Jock Hordern, the Corp film star. *The Horrors of the End Times* is the biggest-budget film ever made by the Corp. It re-creates our country's apocalyptic period with detailed CGI: the global warming that caused the rise of the oceans, the giant walls of fire and the droughts that decimated the land, and the chemical rains that poisoned the rivers. Then the Fourth World Depression came, and the world wars followed. *The Horrors of the End Times* portrays the resilience of the original survivors, a group of just ten thousand people, huddled in a northeastern town, now Zone A. These scenes were actually filmed in the original settlement. It hadn't always been a coastal city, of course—before the global warming events, it was inland a few miles, with a very famous college that educated the richest people in our country, and from all over the world. But after the oceans rose, it became coastal—bordered by the chemical ocean to the east and the badlands to the west. Even here, in the relative safety of the settlement, people collapsed in the street from starvation. Babies died from minor infections because there was little medicine, and plagues tore through the weakened population. Fertility plummeted and has never recovered. Only 5 percent of humans are now capable of having their own children. The Corp decided that the mass fertilization of Breeders would be the only way to maximize reproductive output and prevent humanity dying out. So unless they're part of that 5 percent, the Breeders are surrogates, impregnated with the genes of the fertile.

The Corp also decided that kind of poverty and starvation and war was never going to happen again. It wasn't possible to look after everyone, so they drew a line around the settlement.

The people inside had to sign up to new laws. First—once the borders were set, nobody could go in or out. Second, no government—the World Depressions were caused by government interference, and the best thing was to let the market take care of itself. Third—all decisions were to be based on the principle of what benefits the economy. "Some troublemakers wanted a bill of rights," Jock Hordern pontificates, "but rights were part of the degeneracy, part of the End Times. There are now over five million people inside the Wall. We're the lucky ones."

I honestly couldn't give a shit about the End Times. I mean, I get it—hundreds of years of violence and famine, disease and horror. It was terrible, and it's great that it's over. I'm glad I live in the Corporation. Thank you, dearest overlords. But reciting the same history, over and over, does my head in. I bet my classmates feel the same way, but nobody would ever say that out loud. Like I said before, you never really know who's in contact with the Corp, trying to get extra units by snitching.

I pinch my leg to stay awake.

When the documentary is over, Sir gets us to take turns retelling our understanding of the history. Mathew Anderson begins, repeating the opening of the documentary word for word:

> "After the global environmental disaster came the Fourth World Financial Depression, over a billion people starved to death, which led to a vicious war over the meager resources that remained. Then came the pandemics."

The Corp doesn't say how many years have passed since the initial settlement. I tried to track it through Ma's stories, counting the generations. Her grandmother's grandmother's grandmother was a child then. That girl only survived because she was taken in as a Breeder. The rest of her family was turned away at the border and died of starvation because the Corp already had too many workers. The stages of development, from initial settlement to incorporation to full zoning, must have taken years.

The Crystal withdrawal makes me feel nauseated and sleepy. My stomach lurches, and I pinch my leg again to stay alert.

Mathew Anderson then recalls the Cannibalism of the Innocents—the Corp's way of dealing with a bad harvest one year—which is everyone's favorite scene in *The Horrors of the End Times*, and that makes us all sit up in our seats.

But before Mathew can really get into it, our screens go blank. Sir reads out in a flat voice, "Could everyone turn their attention to the front of the room, and recite the following points, please." It's a mission statement. Our personal computer screens stay blank and the text appears on the big screen at the front of the room.

All over the Corporation, Westies from Zone B to Zone F are stopping what they are doing at this exact moment and are reciting in unison. Only Zone A is exempt, because Zone A is exclusive to the Corp. Reciting our mission statement is meant to help us Westies focus on our goals, make us feel united, and improve our productivity for the Corp. It reminds us where we, as Westies, have come from, and why we do what we do. I don't look at anyone. I just start reading along with everyone else, in as quiet a voice as I can manage without being cited:

"After the End Times, the country's population was decimated. My people of the West found themselves in fire-burned land, unable to live.

"The people of the East pooled their resources and formed a Corporation to survive. My people of the West began their Final Migration to the East. The Corporation generously opened the walls of their settlement to my people of the West.

"My people of the West owe a great debt to the Corporation. As a person of the West, I am eternally grateful to the Corporation. I promise to maximize my units, in order to at least partially repay the Corporation's generosity in hosting me. In good faith, the people of the West will repay the Corp through either work or breeding.

"I promise to uphold the Breeder Laws."

The room is very quiet. Everyone has just said *Breeder* out loud, and it's not a word that you're used to having in your mouth. It's not a word you say in public. Lately, the Corp has stepped up its Breeder campaign; I've noticed the ads on the buses. They only started sending twelve-year-olds to the Incubator last year, and it's still a bit controversial.

Sir is about to say something when the big screen shuts down: it's the end of our school half day and time for us to catch the bus to the desalination plant. I put my mask on and head out the door.

•

"Do I need to light a fire under your ass this evening?" Ma yells from the kitchen. She is a Westie to the core and speaks plainly. Ma is actually my grandmother; nobody except me knows that.

Jessica Meadows is not her real name, and Will Meadows is not my real name, either—they're the names someone put on the fake documents Ma bought the last time we had to move. I don't know Ma's real name, or my mother's; whenever I ask Ma, she says, "What's the point of going into all that? What's past is past." I know that Ma was a Breeder, just like my own mother was.

Ma's at the stove cooking, and it smells awful. Most food now smells awful to me, because of the Crystal 8 withdrawals, but Ma is also a terrible cook.

"Will!" she yells. She wants me to feed our goat, Cranky. Yes, we have a goat. Yes, he is highly illegal, and yet he's only one of the many things in our home that are highly illegal.

"Will!"

I'm sitting at the little fold-up table reading a novel—illegal!—and that's what is really pissing Ma off and is the reason she wants me outside with the goat. Today Ma looks about a hundred years old. No offense. Normally, I think she looks very good for her age; even beautiful for forty-five years old. She's not angry at me because reading novels is illegal—as I said, there are many illegal things going on in our home. Ma can't read or write much, like most Westies, but that isn't the problem either. The problem is that Ma is an extremely practical person, and she thinks reading novels is a massive waste of time, and that I'm too daydreamy and impractical as it is, without "getting lost way up my own ass with a huge bloody book of lies."

Now Ma sighs and gets that deep wrinkle down her forehead. When I see that wrinkle, I get up and put my mask on and go outside without a word.

Cranky bleats at me as he hears the back door and his bell

is ringing—he shakes his head from side to side to really make it bang around. He clangs it when he's irate or happy. I love that sound, and it feels good to be out of the house—even though the chemical fumes in the air hurt my lungs and make my eyes tear up.

Cranky's giving me the evil-goat-eye. "Sorry I'm so late," I say, but he just glares back. He's wearing one of my old rain-coats, which Ma cut up when the last heat wave started. She was scared he'd get sunburnt. I told Ma he didn't need it, that a bit of sun wouldn't bother him. He looks undignified in it, tied around his back with a strange knot sticking up, and this makes me smile as I fill his little pail with bread. I scratch his ears as he eats, and feel his body relax, from the food and the touch. On the way back to the house, I see our tomato plants are bloom-ing. Our garden's illegal too, but it feels good to eat something you've grown yourself, and besides, we need the calories. Like all Westies, we are actually starving, and like everyone else, each day, Ma and I make hard decisions based on units: do we eat a little more, or do we buy extra gas for heating, or, in my case, do we buy my Crystal? Our fruit and veggies are probably full of carcinogens from all the radiation and pollutants, just as the Corp ads warn—so what? Everything's carcinogenic.

I come inside and drop my mask near the door. Then Ma hands me a bowl of food and I make a face. "Don't start," she says, and shoves a fork at me. We sit on the broken-down couch and before I can take a bite, she says, "So. It's not coming."

She means my damn Crystal 8. Ma gets it from a Gray Corps smuggler at the desal plant, and it costs us a fortune. Over the last six months alone, the price has doubled—we've been skip-ping a lot of meals to pay for those pills.

"Maybe they'll come tomorrow," I say, not looking at her, even though I know that's not going to happen.

"You'll need to go out tonight, Will."

"Yeah," I say, meaning *Nah*. I'm not doing it.

"It's been five days already." Her voice is so calm. She could be talking about a shopping trip, rather than going down to the Gray Zone. I've gone there before, of course. But not for over a year.

"I'm okay with waiting another few days," I lie. "The withdrawals aren't that bad." Living without the drugs isn't really an option. Then I think about what the Gray Zone entails, and that doesn't feel like an option either.

She's on her feet and standing in front of me. Damn, she's fast. "I can see the difference in you already."

I feel the heat in my face, and I look away. "Okay. *Okay*. I'll go."

We sit there and eat silently. I manage to swallow my food only because I've made my mind completely blank. When I finish, she says, "Go have a nap first."

•

I take a sleeping pill so I can pass out for a couple of hours. Ma wakes me at midnight, roughly shaking my shoulder. She hands me a shopping bag and leaves. Inside the bag is a new pair of black jeans and a long-sleeved black top—the clothes I wore to the Gray Zone last year are now too small. At least I have my usual thick, black boots. I tie the laces hard. I take my folding knife out of the top drawer but then remember the security post pat-downs and stick it back in the drawer. Ma hobbles back into my room—she broke her right leg badly a long time ago—and gives me an orange and a glass of water and another pill. This one is just a generic painkiller, but it's better than nothing since the withdrawals are now making me ache all over. I swallow the pill, and we walk down the stairs together.

When we get to the front door, Ma looks at me and her eyes are soft, which makes me feel worse.

"Okay?" she says.

I start to shake. It's bloody embarrassing, and I can't stop. I know she sometimes gets scared that I'm not strong enough to get through what's ahead of me. It scares me too. *You need to be as rough as guts in this world, Will*, Ma always says. And yet she's looking at me with those soft eyes.

"Goodspeed, Will. Come home tight and right," Ma says. She makes a sign on her forehead, on her lips, and on her heart. Then she makes the sign on my forehead. She does weird stuff like that sometimes, and mutters little bits of poetry—blessings from the West, I think they are. I shake harder.

Her eyes go steely and she says, "Don't fuck it up. Alright?" That's better—I nod and the shaking stops. I grab my mask and go out the door.

•

I approach security at the Zone F Transit Station, raise my wrist to the scanner, and suck in my breath. I'm waved through without an interrogation. I guess it's because I haven't used any interzone visas for a while—no reason for them to suspect frequent or distant travel. Then I walk slowly through the body scanner and again breathe out with relief when I'm not pulled aside for a pat down.

The security corridor opens out to the massive dome of the

Transit. The perimeter has numbered doors leading to the buses outside, there are escalators going up to a food court, and the ground floor has a few disgusting restaurants and coffee shops. It's crowded and the noise is unreal.

I walk to the east side of the station and, while I wait for the local 42 bus to the Wall, I take a seat on a bench near a café. There's only one other person waiting there—a Shadow, who is very beautiful. Both her Breeder scar and Shadow tattoo are visible, as the laws dictate. I try not to stare at the curl of the embryo brand peeking out from under the tattoo, a red check mark inside a circle. Living in a world comprised almost entirely of men and boys, I'm always entranced when I see a Shadow. Here in the Transit station, there are maybe four hundred people: all of them men and boys, and then there's her. It's not easy to look away. After all, there are only boys and Sir at school; only men and boys at work, apart from two older Shadows who work in the plant's office. Since the Corp only allows Breeders to leave the Incubator either by being bought out or after they've paid off their unit debt through breeding, they usually don't return to the world until they're worn-out Shadows. This Shadow is actually young, or at least she looks young.

The Shadow shifts uncomfortably down the bench. I'm just a skinny kid, but I get why she would see any boy or man as a threat. I don't want her to feel afraid of me—she doesn't deserve that. And Ma would throttle me if she knew I frightened her. Even though it's hard, I try not to stare.

There are never any Breeders in the Transit. I might see a young Breeder—still with her family, under the Incubation age—in public maybe once a year, if that. Families keep Breeders at home because the bounties are so high, even CSOs will kidnap Breeders to sell. I look at the families in line for the buses and all the little kids are boys—most families these days send their Breeders to the Preincubation Program very early on. To be honest, that's what I would do. The unit return is too high to pass up, and besides, it's too risky and expensive to keep them until they're twelve. Then you can invest those saved units into your sons.

There aren't many young guys like me in the Transit either. I'd never squander units by using the Transit outside work or school. It's not worth hanging out with your friends like a Waster when you could be saving units for your future. Ma rolls her eyes at me when I say stuff like that.

"You sound forty years old," Ma says.

"Well, how else will I be able to save up for a house and a Shadow?" I mean, *she's* the one always telling me to be practical.

She looks at me funny. "How do you see *that* happening?"

"It happens," I tell her. "Grandpa bought *you* out of the Incubator, didn't he? I just have to save up."

"It's different for you, Will. Obviously."

"Why?"

She starts to say something, then changes her mind.

"Ma? Say it."

"I was Shadowed a long time ago," is all she says. "Go have fun with your friends."

Friends. I mean, that's another issue.

"I don't want to have fun," I tell her. "I want to save for my future."

Ma snorts and then swears at me in Westie.

The local 42 bus arrives and I get on. It takes about thirty minutes to get to the Wall. It's dark outside, so I can only see my reflection in the bus windows, but I know what's out there—basic, broken-down houses like our neighborhood, just more run-down as we head closer to the Wall. Zone F is the outermost ring of the Corporation, and the zone that the Corp cares least about. It's where Westies are sent when they're first admitted inside the Wall, and where we must stay and work off our first level of unit debt before moving up to the better zones. Its lawlessness is both good and bad, depending on who you are, and what you need.

There are six zones, A to F, spanning out in concentric circles from the Corp center: imagine the golden, domed Zone A in the center, which I have never, ever seen in person—Westies are banned from entering it. The other zones expand from there, with all zones holding a total population of about five million people, across 2,500 square miles. Around the outer boundary of Zone F, there's the Wall. The Wall is the only thing that separates us from the burned-out Great Ocean that's to the east, and the badlands to the north, west, and south.

Ma's people worked themselves up from Zone F to Zone C over several generations, but Ma had to flee Zone C after my mother killed herself. She had no choice but to hide here with me. The alternative was to leave the Corporation altogether, which is never an option. The Great Ocean, which I can see from the desal plant, is a dead body of water with a shiny, thick oil slick across it. Flames break out across the surface spontaneously, sometimes building to a wall of fire that tears across the sea when the southerlies blow. The Corp has sent scientists out, lots of times, to search for signs of life. But there aren't any. There are no fish or sea plants, no life at all. And the Corp has sent exploration crews in all the other directions too, to the rest of our continental land mass—to the north, the south, and the west. Not all come back, but the ones that do describe the dried shell of the world.

The Wall is fiercely guarded because it protects us from the badlands and from the Westies. Just beyond the Wall are *millions* of desperate Westies—some of them have been there for generations—waiting to get in. If security at the Wall broke and all the Westies got through, they'd swarm the Corporation. The delicate systems that keep us alive—the systems that desalinate and purify the ocean water, the aquaculture and hydroponic plants that create nutrition, and that grow protein from our limited and finite supplies, and our basic housing—they would all be overwhelmed. Within weeks, we'd run out of food. Then we'd run out of drinkable water. We'd all die, fast. That's why the Wall has a megapresence of CSOs.

The exception to this airtight security system is the Gray Zone. The Gray Zone hosts one short section of the Wall, a secret and illegal opening that only some people know about, which we call the Gate. It's a gap in the sandstone perimeter of the Wall, about a hundred feet long, bracketed by the usual security posts, except that the CSOs at these posts are really corrupt Gray Corps affiliates. The Gate is porous—it's the only place where Westies can get into the Corporation outside official channels—and a whole ecosystem of activity exists alongside it. This is where I'm heading. The bus lets me out about a mile away, and then I walk down a winding road.

The road opens up to a highway where I can hear the whine of tricked-out cars. It's a Waster playground out here—guys who don't give a shit about saving units, who spend everything they have on their cars, attaching massive speakers or velour seat covers. They go out "hunting," they call it. Reports of missing Breeders and Shadows are mostly due to violent Wasters, who sell them to the Gray Corps or keep them for themselves as prisoners. I stay out of sight of them, behind the trees along the side of the road. I hear drunken shouting and laughter, low voices close by, and my heart starts to race. Alongside the Gray Zone, there's a man-made reservoir. It goes on for miles and, frankly, it terrifies me—Wasters will beat up and kill anyone; they could dump me there and nobody would ever know. I stop at a park at the edge of the reservoir—it's just a length of artificial grass covered in ciggie butts. Next to the park there's a strip of buildings: a 24-7 supply shop, a diner, and at the very end, the security post that leads into the Gray Zone.

I walk up to the post, my stomach cramping. I hate this moment the most, because once I go beyond this point, anything can happen—I won't even have the dubious protection of the CSOs and the Corp Laws.

The window opens as I approach, and I offer up my wrist and wait for the Gray Corps affiliate to scan my chip. He takes thirty units. He's a young guy but heavy, and sweating in the heat. Without a word he comes around and frisks me, reaching into each pocket of my jeans and turning it inside out until he's satisfied I don't have anything of value for him to take. He's slow, and he stinks of breath mints—at least he doesn't go in for a free feel.

"Have a great night, eh?" he says when he's finished, and slaps me on the ass.

"Sure," I say. He starts whistling as he heads back into the booth, because he hasn't realized yet that while he was frisking me, I lifted his gold watch. I've got quick hands—a skill Ma insisted I learn early in life.

There are a lot of Wall Kids here already, and it's only 1:35 a.m. The cars won't start coming till two. The Wall Kids are in small groups, talking and laughing with each other, but they stiffen as

I approach and watch me carefully. Everyone knows everyone down here, and there are strict cliques. Each has its own style—their own code words and jokes, their own tattoos, their own way of dressing and cutting their hair. You need to belong to a clique for your own protection—protection from the Gray Corps, and protection from the other Wall Kids. I've never spent long enough at the Wall to belong to a clique of my own. The Wall Kids live in the Gray Zone—it's their world. They're all undocumented—all off the Grid. I'm not one of them, so I'm a soft target.

I walk up to a clique of four kids that have short, spiky hair that's been bleached completely white and they're wearing tight black jeans and bright blue runners. My heart's banging, and I'm planning to ease things by saying hello or asking them how business has been, what kinds of Gray Corps affiliates have been showing up this week. But as I get close, I change my mind. They're looking with absolute hatred at my black jeans. I'm wearing the same jeans as they are, which means I'm treading on their turf. The kid closest to me, who has a tattoo of a silver gun on his forehead, meets my gaze and says, "Take off your mask and keep your eyes *down*, fuck stick."

I forgot that nobody wears their masks down here—it's important to be able to read people's faces. I pull mine down and drop my eyes and keep walking, hoping I won't start my first night back at the Wall with a gash to the kidneys. Straight away, I start wheezing—the air is so bad. I go past another clique of about seven kids who are all dressed in tight red clothes, but I don't notice anything else about them because I'm careful to look *down* this time. I can feel their hatred radiating at me, so I go past them and three more cliques, until I'm at the other end of the Wall, where there's a kid standing by himself, face mask hanging around his neck, smoking a cigarette. He's short and thin and is wearing a massive, knitted, extremely crazy hat, which has two flaps over his ears. He looks like a total nutter. But when he glances up at me, he's got the most intense and beautiful eyes I've ever, ever seen.

"Hey," I say to the kid.

"Hey, yourself," he says, and sucks on his cigarette. The little face inside the hat is spare and good-looking, with those big eyes and strong cheekbones. He's wearing huge brown corduroys that he's tied up high around his waist with a thick piece of red rope. He's also wearing a sweatshirt and I can see he's got a few layers under that. We essentially have two seasons—unbearably hot, and unbearably hot with torrential rain. Some years we have a short winter of a month or so, when it gets down to maybe forty degrees. Anyway, he must be boiling in there—just looking at him makes me want to itch. Maybe his Gray Corps contact gave him these clothes? This place attracts the extremely rich, people who can afford to be weird.

The kid offers me his cigarette and I take a puff and pass it back to him and he sees my hands, which are shaking again. "First time?" he says.

"No," I say. He waits for me to explain, but I don't say anything. It's better if everyone minds their own fucking business in the Gray Zone.

"Yeah," he says, and shakes his head. "You never know what sort of ugly you're going to get down here, do you?" His accent's strong Westie—even stronger than Ma's.

"I'm Alex," he says, holding out his hand.

"Will," I say, and take his hand. As I do, I realize that the kid is not a regular kid, but a fucking *Breeder*, and suddenly the layers of clothes make sense. It takes my breath away. I don't know how I know, because it isn't obvious—she's even skinnier than I am, and you can't see that she has breasts or curves or anything under all those layers—but somehow, I know. Then I notice the edge of a scar, a dark curl, on the right side of her face, partly hidden by one of the crazy hat-flaps. I can't see the whole thing, but I'm sure it's the edge of her Breeder mark. They brand it onto all of them in the Incubators. Ma has one below her Shadow tattoo. My mother would have had one. The Breeder sees me realize and drops my hand, jumping back, like I've given her an electric shock. What she's doing is so dangerous—living as a boy, when she's so easily discoverable as a Breeder. It's not only Wasters who will trade Breeders to the Gray Corps or kidnap them for their own uses. Plus, she's so young that there's no way she's been discharged from the Incubator—she's either been bought out or she's run away. But nobody who's been bought out would be down at the Wall looking for work from random Gray Corps affiliates. And if she'd been bought out, she'd have a Shadow tattoo, so she must have run away, which means there's a callout for her and if she's caught, she'll get sent straight to the Rator. I can't help admiring her. At the same time, I feel a smack of disgust, deep in my stomach—I just touched a fucking *Breeder*.

"It's okay," I say quietly, and she looks me in the eyes, and I watch her trying to decide whether it is or isn't okay. I'm actually not sure either. I hold her gaze steady, wanting to show her that she's safe with me. Meanwhile, she's dropped her cigarette. "Ah, fuck," she says, and reaches into her pocket. Then she drops the pack on the ground as well.

"I'll get it," I say, and pick up the pack and light her a new cigarette. I hold it out to her and as she takes it, our fingers touch and I flinch. Our eyes meet again. She looks terrified. I wonder how long she's been surviving outside the Incubator.

"Light one for yourself," she says, so I do. Then we lean against the Wall, side-by-side, smoking. And trying to calm down. I want to say something but there's nothing to say. We just stand there with our backs against the Wall and smoke our lungs out.

A few minutes later, a large black car with Corp plates and gold trim pulls up in front of us. The number plate says MR. GOLDBAGS. Ah, for fuck's sake. "Well, here's my ride," Alex says and winks at me, then waves at the driver, whose face is like a pink smudge through the tinted glass. "Goodspeed to you, Will," she says.

"You too."

Alex's eyes look sad. There's something flint-strong there too, as if she'd at least *try* to break your ass if you crossed her, which cheers me up a bit—but as I watch her walking, smiling hard, toward the car, what I mainly see is how small and skinny she is, her stick legs lost in the corduroys. Then she opens the passenger door and climbs inside without looking back.

•

It's 2:15 a.m. and I'm still waiting in the same spot, feeling desperate. There's nothing about me that makes me stand out. I'm a tall beanpole—I don't look particularly athletic, or like I'd be a good fighter. I don't even have proper sass. I have one hand on my hip, staring out at middle space, my eyes narrowed like a hard-ass, and I feel really fucking stupid, but it's honestly the best I can do. I've only ever done Breeder running in the Gray Zone—for that, they want kids who can dodge in and out of crowds, get into little spaces, and who can move *fast, fast, fast*—but I've grown about six inches in the last year so maybe I don't look the part anymore. You never know what the Gray Corps is looking for down at the Wall, and I hate *talking* to Gray Corps affiliates, let alone marketing myself to them. Plus, what the Gray Corps is searching for out here changes all the time, and it's hard for me to read what's hot at the moment—I'm not at the Wall often enough. Gray Corps affiliates may want sex, drug couriers, Breeder running, and who knows what else. Since there are always so many more Wall Kids than Gray Corps affiliates, the market is theirs and they can be choosy. Gray Corps guys want that extra thing, that unnameable thing, that something that will enhance their personal brand. I just don't have it, I reckon. They want cool kids, hot kids, kids who represent their rich, powerful image, because their corrupt Corp colleagues will be watching and judging them, and hell, personal image and branding *always* matter.

Most cars don't even slow down to give me a proper look. To prove my point, a silver convertible drives by me and then brakes in front of a clique, dressed in cutoffs and flip-flops, with shark tattoos on their cheeks. The smallest kid is backflipping in front of the group and when the passenger door of the convertible opens, he gets inside. I hear a car horn sound and turn to see a gold SUV pulled up in front of me.

The dark glass of the driver's window slides down just a little. I can't see the driver's face because the interior lights are off. The car's plates are Corp, they're painted gold: ROB #1. *Excellent*. The car's a giant, revamped vintage, priceless probably, and while you get all sorts of rich at the Wall, this car is causing a stir, with the shark-tattoo kids throwing me filthy looks.

I can tell they're wondering why the fuck a Gray Corps affiliate with that car would go after me, and I'm wondering that myself.

Rob #1 is waiting for me to speak. I don't say anything—Ma rightly taught me that the person who speaks first loses. I make myself stare right back through the reflective window, not blinking, even though I can't see his face and my damn knees are shaking.

He clears his throat. "Money or drugs?" His voice sounds middle-aged, fat, and rich. Big surprise.

Then the interior lights flick on and I see the top of his face. He raises his eyebrows. But I still don't say anything. The driver's window comes down all the way.

He isn't middle-aged and he isn't fat—he's only about thirty, and he's lean and good-looking. In fact, he's fucking hot. I can smell his expensive aftershave and the leather interior of his gorgeous car and part of me is thinking that he *is* excellent, and wishes I were him; I wish I were Rob #1—which makes me really hate myself.

"Crystal 8," I say, keeping my voice as steady as I can. I used to just about vomit every time I asked for Crystal 8 down here, certain that I'd be reported to the Corp, or bashed and dumped somewhere. Raped first. The secret truth is, most Gray Corps affiliates *love* hiring Crystal 8 boys: the rareness of me, the thrill in the risk. But there's no hint of fear or anxiety in Rob's eyes. He openly and slowly looks me over, from head to toe, and raises his eyebrow again. I'm clearly not what he thought I was. He doesn't say anything, and I realize he's waiting for me to make an offer. I just lift my chin and stare at him harder. I'm not fucking going to: it's the first rule of negotiation to get the other person to make the first offer. Any five-year-old in Zone F will tell you that.

He nods at me. "Crystal 8 is very difficult to get at the moment," he says. "Is there anything else you'd trade for?" My stomach turns over. Ma and I have heard that Crystal 8's no longer available. That CSOs are, finally, for real, cracking down on all the Gray markets—on drugs, on Breeder running, on everything—and that they're sending people straight to the Rator if they're caught. Not only Westies, even Gray Corps affiliates themselves. If that's the truth, then I'm truly fucked. I feel a sharp wave of nausea.

"I don't need anything else," I tell him.

I turn to go, and he says, "Hang on. I said it's difficult, not *impossible*."

Fucking asshole. I face him. "So can you get me some, or what?"

"You're not big on charm, are you?" he says.

I shrug. Charm is for the Corp.

"I can get it for you," he says, smiling.

Fucking sadistic Gray Corps fucker. Rob is probably highly ranked within his legit Corp life, with his lovely golden car and his easy access to Crystal 8—and what else? Electronic elephants, probably, if he wants them. Skiing holidays on imaginary mountains. Swimming at digital beaches where you can taste the salt. Or maybe—who knows?—the Corp has access to the real thing.

Then he says, "I'll give you a week of Crystal and fifty units for four hours. Breeder running."

I wish I could tell him to go fuck himself, but I need the Crystal so bad. He's still holding my gaze, and I don't see a bit of shame in his eyes. Those big eyes are telling me that even when what he wants to do is so wrong, he's the one with the power. I'm the one who wants to die with fear and shame. "For that, you only get an hour of Breeder running," I tell him.

He snorts. The dark window of the car goes up and he starts the engine. I just stand there, holding my ground. He's bluffing. He might be calm and confident as anything, while my face is burning and my hands are shaking, but I could see something in him: there's a quality about me that he wants, that he thinks will be useful.

And then he drives off, slowly moving away from me. Fuck. *Fuck.* It's 2:27 a.m. I'm close to caving, close to pathetically running after his evil, beautiful car, when he hits the brakes.

The window comes down again and his hand reaches out. A big hand, with curly hair on the knuckles. He points back at me. *"Two* hours," he says. "Get in."

He's pissed off, which makes me feel really pleased, and only goes to prove that I am a moron: it's mental to piss off anyone who is about to have you locked inside his car. But I can't stand the thought of not holding something back, some kind of keeping of myself.

I run up to his car and get into the back seat, still stupidly elated. As the door slams shut, I hear the click of the central locking.

He revs down the road a mile, the car like a graceful animal, and then we hit the back of the line of expensive Corp cars. Rob brakes. We could be here for a long time—I can't even see the front of the line. I've got a while to think about what might lie ahead.

As we're waiting, the phone rings and Rob answers it on speaker. "They say it's going to take another hour to get the Grid down," the voice says. "So we're going to run a game. Do you want your Westie to fight?" In between Breeder runs, the Gray Corps often fight us for bets. I've only ever done fist fights, but I've heard they sometimes arm kids with knives, even guns.

Rob sniffs. "Nope. I need my Westie to be in good form."

Awesome.

He looks at me in the rearview mirror.

I look back at him and nod.

When we reach the parking lot at the Gate, we park beside a silver sedan and get out. The Gate is just a hundred-yard gap in the Wall with electrified fencing, facing the badlands, with flood lights and cameras. It's so bright, I can't see beyond the fence, but I can hear the roar of millions of Westie refugees, just feet away from me.

I just stand there, looking out, as Rob talks to his cronies. They say the badlands are barren for as far as you can go—hot and bleak nothingness. I've heard there may be other cities, but it would take you more than a lifetime of walking to reach them, if you could somehow keep yourself alive through the windswept landscape and the chemical fires and the acid rain. The land is dead from the bushfires that tore through, and the lakes and rivers are poisoned. Ma says her people used to live near forests before the trees died, but that was hundreds of years ago.

The job of Breeder runners is to smuggle healthy Breeders into the Incubator so that their Gray Corps affiliate can get a lot of money—like, *a lot* of money. Enough for Rob to buy another fancy car for every night of Breeder running he does. There are twenty or so adrenaline-filled Wall Kids jumping around me with their Gray Corps affiliate standing calmly by. We're all waiting for the flood lights to switch off and the electrified gate to open. Closest to me are a shark tattoo kid and a red outfit kid. They glare at me and I glare back because we're competing for the best Breeders. If we get to them first, we'll get bonuses. I look around for Alex, wondering if she's a runner too, but I can't see her anywhere.

Rob shoves two photos in front of me. "They need to look as

close to these two as possible," he says, pointing, and I almost laugh in his fucking face. One of the photos is of a Breeder aged fourteen or fifteen. The other one is even younger than that. Except they look like no Breeders I've ever seen. Only Corp or maybe Gray Corps look like that: their skin is clear; they're slightly plump; and their eyes are unclouded. I don't need to go outside the gate to tell Rob that there will be nobody out there who looks close to that. We Westies inside the Wall are thin and starved and sick-looking; the people outside will be doing much worse.

"They *must* look as close to this as possible," Rob says seriously. "And check their eyes." He means for disease.

"Okay."

"Make sure you fucking check!"

"I will!"

"You have twelve minutes, then they lock you out."

I nod.

He shoves a baggie of small gold nuggets in my hand. There's an arrangement where they shut down the Grid for twelve minutes at a time, but no longer, so that the Gray Zone doesn't show up as anything strange on the mainframe Corp security system. Like the whole Gray economy, parts of the Corp know about Breeder running—they're just paid to look the other way. *Sure, hasn't the whole world always run on dodgy deals?* Ma always says. *You can do or get whatever you like if you have the units.*

•

We line up, jostling each other, along the perimeter of the Gate. I hear a whistle, which means the Gray Corps guards have been paid off and left their posts. Then the flood lights switch off. The electrified fence is still closed. The moon is up, and what I can see through the wire is miles and miles and *miles* of people. I can see orderly lines of tents and other shoddy structures. I can see small gas stoves burning. I wonder what they eat out here. The Westies can buy goods from the Gray Corps when they have gold or things to trade, but they say they grow their own scrubby vegetables and also hunt a type of small, hardy rodent that managed to outlast the End Times.

In the moonlight, the faces of the people look particularly desperate. They'd prefer to trade with the Gray Corps than go with the official Breeder Selections. They say there are over fifty million people outside the Wall, and every year the Corporation lets in six thousand. The Corp used to sponsor the Breeder's whole family, but they don't want all that surplus life anymore, so the families just get to nominate one other person for entry besides the Breeder. The Corp throws the Breeder's family a handful of units, but it's nothing like the value of the gold they'll get from the Gray Corps tonight.

No matter how hard I find life under the Corp, I always know that there's this—the badlands—and it's much, much worse out there. At the end of the day, I'm lucky to be a Westie who lives within the Corporation rather than outside the Wall. I can barely look at the Westies' faces.

There's another whistle and the Gate opens. Rob punches my back and shouts, "Go, go, go, go, go!" I run forward with the other Wall Kids, shoving Shark Tattoo out of my way.

At the same time, thousands of Westies hurtle toward us. It's terrifying, you can feel their despair and their fear, and I'm scared they're going to crush us.

I weave through the crowd. The idea is not to attract too

much attention, but even though I'm not a sleek, pink-cheeked Corp, I look comparatively healthy and bright-eyed next to all these people who are bony and ashen from malnutrition. No matter how I try to blend in, they all know who I am, and why I'm here. A ripple goes through the crowd. People start holding up their children and pushing them at me. A man with the most tired eyes shoves a tiny Breeder in my face. "Here! Take her! *Take* her!"

My body revolts as I take her in my arms. I'm holding a Breeder. She's small and only around twelve years old. I fight more revulsion as I brush her hair back from her forehead and look at her eyes—cloudy, diseased. "No," I say, handing her back and forcing him out of my way.

Another Breeder is quickly thrust in front of me. I pull back her hoodie and check her eyes. Healthy. She's skeletal.

"I'll take her," I say.

The man holding her is very old and very thin. His eyes are kind and full of tears. "Thank you," he says. Maybe he doesn't know what's going to happen to his daughter or granddaughter when she goes beyond the Wall to the Incubator. But he probably does. Another child huddles behind him; maybe that child is lucky—maybe that child is a boy.

"Papa!" the Breeder cries, as Papa pushes her at me, and I pick her up; she's trembling. She wails and buries her face into my chest—I'm torn between disgust and pity. I open the baggie and shove some gold—not much—into Papa's scrawny hand.

Next, I choose a taller Breeder, sullen but beautiful. I grab her wrist and she kicks me. Her mother comes up to her, boxes the side of her head, and tells her to be polite. I give her mother some gold and she nods, neither happy nor sad.

The Breeder looks away as she offers me her hand. I take it.

Then, with one Breeder in my arms, and dragging the other tightly by the hand, I sprint back to the Wall.

•

I run five times that night, and smuggle twelve Breeders into the Corp. Some of them are clearly under twelve years old. Toward the end of the agreed two hours, I help Rob process them. He opens the back door of his SUV and we line them up alongside it. As I give them green pills—sedatives that will keep them quiet for the long drive into the heart of the Corporation—they're all sobbing except for the tall, sullen one. She spits the pill onto the ground and Rob steps forward, gets her in a headlock, and pinches her nose. I pick the pill off the ground, hesitate. Rob shouts, "Hurry the fuck up!" My hands shaking, avoiding eye contact, I push the pill into her mouth.

I tell the Breeders to get into the back of the SUV, one by one. The smallest Breeder drops something—a dirty, stuffed rabbit. I pick it up and give it back to her and she says, "Thank you." She starts crying and I say, "Shhh," looking behind me, scared that Rob will hit her. The tall Breeder glares at me, then turns to the little one and talks to her quietly. I tell them all to lie down, faceup, with their arms by their sides. When they don't understand, I act it out. Then I carefully wrap them in blankets. The tall, sullen one pushes my hands away and, as she tucks herself in, I see she has a massive purple bruise around her eye. Then I stack lighter blankets on top of them, even on top of their faces, followed by light packing boxes on top of the blankets. I position the boxes carefully, avoiding their heads, but the blankets have to cover their faces. I know that, sometimes, Breeders suffocate like this. I can hear the tall Breeder singing to the little ones in Westie: a low, sad lullaby that Ma used to sing to me. Finally, I slam the back door closed and lock it, and give Rob the keys. I get into the back seat and we drive in silence. There's no longer any traffic so it only takes five minutes. The Breeders in the back of the car are whispering to each other.

When we reach the point at the Wall where Rob picked me up, he parks the car. He turns and raises his hand and transfers units onto my chip. "There's your tip." I look at the tiny screen in my wrist: two hundred units.

Then he gives me a vial of pills. "That's a week's supply of Crystal 10," he says. "It's much better than your usual Crystal 8 shit."

He holds up a bottle of booze. "You want this too?"

"Nah," I say. I hate drinking—the alcohol messes with my condition and makes me vom my guts out. Then he holds up another, much smaller bottle, and I see the logo of a white cloud. Memo. This time I nod and hold out my hand, and he tips three light-blue pills into my palm. Memo is for peace and forgetting. Finally, he hands me a little bag of gold pieces. Ma will be happy to have ready cash.

"Enjoy," he says.

It's dawn as Rob drives off and I walk away from the Gray Zone with Crystal 10, two hundred units, a bag of gold, the security guard's watch, and a job. I'm going to meet Rob at the Wall every Tuesday night from now on. I exit the security gate just as Goldbags's car pulls up and Alex jumps out—she looks tired. We're happy to see each other but also awkward, staring at each other as we stand in the street in the early morning light. She points at the greasy diner on the other side of the road. "Do you want to get coffee with me?"

My heart pounds. "Next time?" I say. "I'm just so . . . eviscerated."

We look at each other.

"So I have to ask," Alex begins. "You weren't off Breeder running or anything, were you?" She laughs.

I laugh too. "What? No! As if!" I lie. "Drugs." I hold up my haul of Crystal 10. It just looks like any drug baggie—lots of Westies do drug runs for the Gray Corps.

She smiles. "Gotcha. Cool."

We look at each other again.

"What about you?" I ask. "Were *you* Breeder running?"

"No, I run drugs too," she says, and I can tell she's also lying.

"Cool," I say.

"Well . . . see ya," she says. She turns to go.

"Wouldn't wanna be ya . . ." I say. I start to head off, then stop. Part of me wants to spend time with her, but . . . she's a Breeder. It's too dangerous. I turn to wave at her but she's already striding across the road. I stand there and wait, watching as she opens the door to the diner. But she goes inside and doesn't turn back.

•

I let myself into the house just as the pink is leaving the sky, and just as the Memo is wearing off, giving me a hangover of jitters and regret. When I open the door, Ma is sitting right in the foyer on a kitchen stool, her face pale with fear. "Alright?" she says.

"Yeah, Ma. Alright," I say, my jaw so tense with self-disgust and anger, I can barely speak. I tear my mask off, and Ma grabs my hand and I hold onto her, tight. But then I feel guilty and pull away. Her eyes are determined, and also full of sorrow. They're the same eyes that I saw on so many Breeder kids during the night. I don't have to make her feel worse. She knows.

I hold out the vial of Crystal 10 to show her and transfer 150 units to her chip. I give her all the gold pieces and the watch.

She nods. "Good."

"I'd better have a shower," I say.

I go upstairs to the bathroom. I tear off my clothes and shove them in the laundry basket. I'd set them on fire, except that I'll need them next week. I take a Crystal 10 and chuck the rest into the top drawer of the vanity and step into the shower, turning on just the hot tap. I hate my body. I hate having a body. Ideally, I would just float above the world, but every day I have to fight to keep this body. I trace the scar down my side, from when I fell on a sharp piece of machinery at work. I have another scar, very faded, down my arm, from when I was a little kid. As Westies, our bodies are sick, failing machines: we're only allowed to keep them alive if we pump more and more units into the Corp, and to do that, we have to wear them out. I have to fight even harder than other Westies to keep this body, and after just days without Crystal, I can see differences. Despite my emaciation, there's a new softness around my hips and stomach. And around my chest. I shiver. Other people might not notice, but Ma's right—I got the Crystal just in time. I can still see the Breeders lying in the back of the SUV, and I shut my eyes tight. I stand under the water, scrubbing and scrubbing my skin with the washcloth, watching it get red and burnt, stinging. Good.

When I'm finished, I get into my old baggy jeans and hoodie, set my alarm, and scrunch up on my bed: just a twenty-minute nap until I need to get ready for work.

Ma's knocking at the door. "Can I get you anything?" she calls. I don't answer.

"Will?" I can hear her heavy breathing; I can hear the cane tapping the floor, the cane that she only uses when she's exhausted.

"Will? Are you okay?" she sounds worried. She never sounds worried.

I clench my teeth. "I'm okay, Ma," I say, as gently as I can.

There's silence, then I hear a sliding sound and see that she's slipped a chocolate bar and some gold pieces under my door. I hear her walking off; the quick, uneven sound of her bad leg. I know all this isn't her fault. I know she's trying to protect me, and that she would do anything for me—has done—and there's nothing else she can do. I just hate myself so, so much.

•

On the way to work, I visit the Book Shadow. I go down a maze of streets, into the narrow lanes of the Old Town. I walk up to the ratty wooden door that says *Knife Sharpener* on it and I hold my wrist up to the sign until the security scanner beeps me in. I instantly feel something inside me relax. It's a large, light-filled room, covered with ye olde furniture and doilies, and laid out carefully on shelves and tables are real, printed books. Things from the old times, before they had the entertainment plug.

On one wall there's a painting with angels and devils, which people used to believe in. The devils grimace in pain, while the angels look happily upward, to a place known as Heaven. The

Book Shadow has a collection of heavy books containing photos and paintings of things I've never, ever seen in person—forests and beaches, bridges and rivers and waterfalls. She keeps them in a private room and brings them out sometimes for me to look at. Ice caps. Fjords. Whales. Elephants, zebras, parrots—creatures the Corporation says don't exist anymore, outside their quality simulations in Zone A. Inside the Corporation there are only the animals we can eat—chickens, cows, and pigs. A few contraband goats, like Cranky.

I take the novel I just finished out of my backpack and touch its pages before I put it back on the shelf. You can buy books, or swap them, or pay a loan fee. I half don't want to let go of this novel, but I never let myself keep any of them. It's about a guy named Holden Caulfield who's my age and lives under a super-rich Corporation. He drops out of his rich school—it isn't clear why—and then he travels around on a train and goes to a Corporate City called New York. I love that name. He gets really sad in a big, rich park that he used to go to when he was little, and then he gets really sad in a rich museum that he used to go to when he was little, and then he thinks about his dead brother and how sad his family is. To be honest, I don't know why he's so sad—he's rich, gets to go to school, doesn't have to work, and there's no mention of anyone monitoring his units. I mean, he lives before the End Times so he can basically do whatever he wants. If he were alive today, he'd be considered a Mood and he'd be given some pills, then the Corporation would calculate what he's cost society through his mental issues and he'd have to pay that balance with money or time, and that would be the end of it. Unless, of course, he reached the point where his unit debt to the Corporation got too big to pay off, in which case he'd be sent to the Rator. Holden just goes on and on about how sad he is, and about all the things that make him sad. For hours. Days. *Weeks*. But I still like him. He's alive in the times when there were cities called New York and Paris and London, when there were underground subways, and shopping centers that anyone could go to, and restaurants where you could eat pretty much what you wanted. And *parks*. You could hang out in a park for an afternoon feeling sad and not even have any units deducted *because nobody was keeping track*. Nobody cared whether you were adding value to your Corporation or not. Nobody was concerned if you sat there like a pudding for years, generating a massive unit debt and risking the collapse of life as we know it! In fact, nobody even *knew* if you were racking up your unit debt because nobody even bothered calculating it.

For a long time, entertainment was against the Laws in the Corp—using resources for mere pleasure meant robbing others of their chance to eat. But then the Corp got wealthier and the econometrics department did studies that showed people were more efficient if they were given entertainment. Now we all have the entertainment plug in our arms, to watch vids and stuff, and we can also use it to text. It's very efficient, because the stimulus goes directly into your senses—sight, sound, taste, whatever you like. The newest version can predict your desires—it scans the flashes in your brain cortex to see how you're feeling. If you're happy, say, it knows that if that happiness continues you'll tip over into boredom, so what you need is a bit of tension and sadness. The plug then sends you some gentle melancholy—it might upload a sad love story with an ambivalent ending, and after you watch the vid you feel grateful for your own life.

Personally, I prefer stories from the olden days, even though you can't control them, and you never know how they'll make you feel. I've read eight books altogether since I discovered the Book Shadow—all illegal, all strange and beautiful.

I run my finger along the book spines, trying to feel a tug from a particular book. What I always look for is a good first sentence. I take out a scruffy, slim volume. "Mrs. Dalloway said she would buy the flowers herself." Nope. I put it back. The next: "Edward helped me into his car, being very careful of the wisps of silk and chiffon, the flowers he'd just pinned into my elaborately styled curls, and my bulky walking cast." God, no. I put this one back and run my hand along the next shelf. My fingers catch on a particularly beaten-up book and I take it out: "It was Napoleon who had such a passion for chicken that he kept his chefs working around the clock." Cool.

Sometimes the Book Shadow comes in and her face is all lit up and she tells me what I should read next. She'll run around and say, "You've *got* to read this! No, read this, this! You would *love* it!" and I get excited too. Sometimes she never appears—I just choose what I want and scan her some units and leave.

The Book Shadow has never told me her name. I've been coming here for a year now, and she tells me about the people who painted the pictures and wrote the strange novels. She knows all about so-called seers and visionaries and artists who lived hundreds of years ago. To be honest, they sound like Moods—but the things they made are so beautiful. She tells me that most of these old things have been lost forever. The Book Shadow is so different from other Shadows—she has this amazing store, and she runs her own life. Westie males can buy out Shadows and then they can theoretically have their own children—that is, if it's physically possible. Or Breeders pay off their own debt through breeding, and get a regular Corp job, but not before their forties. The Book Shadow is probably twenty years old, and it costs about five of Rob's vintage golden SUVs to buy out a twenty-year-old Breeder from the Corp. Maybe she escaped from the Incubator? Or maybe someone did buy her out. The Book Shadow reminds me of Alex—Alex would love it here. Maybe one day I can bring her here and show her these books. She and the Book Shadow would get on so well. I feel my face get hot—what am I thinking? It would be mental to take Alex outside the Gray Zone.

I hear a soft click and then footsteps—there are all kinds of secret doors and levers in this place. I don't know how the Book Shadow has managed to keep her shop under the radar, but she has, and does.

The footsteps stop close by.

"Hello?" I whisper. "It's just me. It's Will."

Her head comes around the corner, and then she's standing there. She's wearing track pants and her hair is matted.

"Hello, Will," she says. She looks terrible, but her eyes are bright, her voice thick. The red Shadow tattoo is vivid over her Breeder scar, not dull like Ma's.

"Hello," I say. "How are you?"

She smiles and shrugs. "Oh. You know." She sees the book in my hand. "Do you want me to choose another book for you?"

"Yes, please."

She turns and runs her hand down the spines of the books on the top shelf. Her hand falls on something and she gives it to me—its pages are worn and soft, and I can smell the paper and my heart just kind of sighs. *"Pride and Prejudice,"* she tells me. "It's very, very old, and very good."

"Is it set in New York?" I say, stroking the pages.

"No," she says. "It's set in England, on the other side of the world from New York. It's about a family of five daughters—five!—who live in a house with their parents and all want to get married. They live in a huge house in the countryside and go to parties and have friends over for tea. It's totally wild."

"'Daughters'?"

"Like Breeders," she said. "Except they don't have to breed."

Mind. Blown.

The Book Shadow looks happy. Before I can stop myself, I ask her something I've always wanted to ask. "I love this shop. How did you find it? Did somebody give it to you?" I just blurt it out. I'm not used to talking to Shadows, and she makes me nervous.

She hesitates, then nods.

"Was it the same person who bought you out of the Incubator?"

She stares at me as though I've said something unbelievably cruel. Her face darkens and becomes very red. She turns away. "I'll see you next time, Will," she says quietly, and shuffles away from me.

I'm shaking and cursing myself. I carefully wrap the book in an old T-shirt and put it in the bottom of my backpack. Then I hold up my wrist to the scanner set in a wooden box with an owl carved on the top and transfer thirty units. I stand there and close my eyes and take a deep breath, inhaling the scent of old things, of old pages. I hear the soft click of a hidden door and know she's gone. Then I let myself out. The door shuts behind me with a *wssht* and I wonder whether the shop will be here when

I come again. Every now and then you hear of the Corp raiding shops, and all the treasures get sent to the Corporation Recycling Center to be turned into milk cartons. The owners go to the Rator.

It's sunny in the street, and I still don't want to get on the work bus, so I stop by a Corporation flower shop, and buy two bunches of proper regulation roses, which cost a bomb. But Rob tipped me a bomb, so I'm going to bring some flowers to Melissa and Belinda.

•

I get on the bus and activate the entertainment plug. It's too dangerous to take out my new book—chances are there's a CSO or just a regular, lowlife snitch on the bus. I scan the home screen and feel a flicker of pleasure when I find a new horror film in the Night Clown series—I find horror really comforting. I settle back for the hour-long bus ride to the other side of Zone F.

Before the film loads, I have to sit through the compulsory Corp ad—well, it's an "optional" ad, but I get five units for watching it, and if I don't watch it, it's noted on my permanent record.

The ad opens by panning across the landscape of Zone C: the new Transit station, the gigantic shopping center, the glass office buildings. Everyone in Zone F talks about living in Zone C as their life's dream, even though realistically, they will be happy if their kids one day live and work in Zone E—their sons will get there through hard work, and their Breeders through serv- ing time in the Incubator. We're allocated one visit a month to Zone E, to explore and dream. We only get once-yearly passes to visit Zones D and C, and a life in Zone C is the sort of goal achievable by one in ten thousand Zone F families—through random, stupid good luck. Zone B is out of reach for us, and for our progeny, and we're not allowed to visit. When Ma and her family lived in Zone C, they were given passes to visit Zone B and they aspired to move there—it's the apex of Westie achievement. Westies are not allowed in Zone A at all, for any reason. We hear things about it—the amazing hospitals, facilities, and *universities*. From the plant on the clearest days, I can see the glittering dome that covers Zone A. It filters their air and I've heard they don't even need to wear masks in there, but nobody really knows for sure.

The ad focuses on a family standing at the front door of a broken-down Zone F apartment: a Shadow, a man, and a small boy. The voiceover begins, recognizable immediately as Jock Hordern:

> *"The generosity of the Corporation led to Shadow Stevens being accepted within the Wall as a Breeder when she was fourteen years old. Through her hard work, Shadow Stevens produced seventeen live births at the Incubator. Then, Mr. Stevens Shadowed her with his hard-earned unit savings and they started their own family."*

Shadow Stevens waves at the camera.

> *"The minimum age to send Breeders to the Incubator has gone DOWN! Unit bonuses for Breeders are UP! What does that mean for Zone F families just like yours?"*

The camera zooms in on the man.

"We were more than happy to put our eight-year-old Breeder into a Preincubation Program, for the good of the Corporation. We no longer carry the debt of raising a Breeder, and we've been given a bonus of nineteen thousand units that we can use to educate our son!"

The small boy is smiling. There's no sign of their Breeder, who's presumably already in her Preincubation Center. The man speaks.

"With these units, the dream of our descendants getting into Zone C is becoming a reality! Thanks, Corporation!"

The small boy makes the thumbs-up sign.

"Thanks, Stevens Family! The Corp's new, generous plan is good for all of us, in every zone—more live births make us all more viable. And it's especially good for Zone F families like the Stevenses, because they can earn enough to make their dreams come true even faster! Early Incubation will give them nineteen thousand units and that will benefit them for generations to come. You're doing the right thing, Stevens family!"

The camera pans out as the whole Stevens family— except the Breeder—waves and smiles and says together: *"Thanks, Corporation! Our dream is a reality!"*

One day, I would love to have a family, even though Ma says that's a dangerous and impossible plan for me. For most Westies it's impossible—95 percent of people are infertile. So even those Westies who manage to save enough units to buy a Shadow from the Incubator have a very small chance of a living child. It's strange, though—even though it's so impossible, I can guarantee that if you ask any Westie, they'll tell you that *this* is the dream that keeps them going. *This* is the dream that keeps them grinding through every hour of back-breaking, mind-crushing work: the dream of something better for another generation, for some future person who is connected to you, even if it's just in your imagination. Otherwise, how would we get through each day? I always thought of Ma as the least sentimental person I ever met, but once she came home from work and I watched as she emptied her bag onto the kitchen table, like she did every day. She pointed to a certificate she'd received—some sad prize for cleanest factory drone of the month, or something, which came with a ten-unit bonus—and rolled her eyes. I picked it up to chuck it into the trash bin when I noticed some loose, crumpled pages stuck behind the certificate—several kid's drawings, done in crayon and colored pencil. She snatched them from me and clutched them to her chest.

"What are they?" I asked her.

"Nothing," she said.

"Ma!"

"Okay, fine. They're drawings you and your mother did when each of you were small."

"And you carry them around with you?"

"Yes."

"Why?"

She sniffs.

"Ma. Why?"

"I look at them sometimes. To cheer myself up. Now go and feed that goat."

•

I raise my wrist to the security scanner and get beeped inside, then ride the elevator to the Admin Center at the top of Desal Tower 4 to get my work allocation. When the elevator doors open, I see other guys with flowers, standing around and chatting. Behind them are enormous ceiling-to-floor windows—to the east, I can see the vast, dead ocean. Today, the chemical fires flaring across the surface of the water are bigger than usual because of the dry-season winds.

The thing to do on Wednesday mornings is to bring a bunch of flowers to the office Shadows. Melissa, who's around thirty, has only recently been bought out of the Incubator, and Belinda, who's Ma's age. On the whole, I *much* prefer Belinda. Both of them have curling Breeder scars on their cheeks underneath their Shadow tattoos. Belinda's partner, Simon, is a Westie who works high up in the desalination plant and they're both saving units to pass on to Belinda's nephew. Belinda and Simon can't have any live births themselves.

Melissa has a number of serious admirers. A lot of guys my age down at the plant have a crush on Melissa, which is *mental* because there's no way that Melissa would even *look* at us seriously. After all, she is with a senior Westie at our plant who has a house, a car, and a lifetime of units to give her. But Melissa accepts our offerings anyway.

There's already a garden of flowers on Melissa's desk: mostly pink geraniums from the flower man who sells them at the front gates, the stems wrapped in foil. I feel pretty happy to have proper roses with me. Behind the flowers, Melissa is beaming. "Are those for me, beanpole?"

I smile. "Morning, Melissa. Yep!" I quickly give one of the bunches to her, and then cross the room to Belinda's desk.

Belinda waves at me. "Hello, handsome. Am I going to have to put out for those flowers?"

"Maybe," I tell her. "But first, could you tell me which section I'm working in today?"

"Hmmm," she says and starts tapping at her keyboard. "Where do you want to work?" she asks, pretending that I have a choice.

I sigh. "Oh, I don't care. Just not somewhere butt-ugly."

She stops typing and looks at me above her spectacles. "Oh, honey. Every section here is butt-ugly."

She's so right. Belinda is awesome because, when she can, she gives me a temporary job above my station. I'm great with electronics and systems, so sometimes she gets me to help with that—setting things up, or troubleshooting—rather than doing another boring shift watching a desal machine run. My work clearance is officially for the lowest rung of plant work—it's so dull, I wish I could be anesthetized for eight hours a day, that the Corp would just use my mind and body without me being aware of it.

"Also," Belinda says, "did you hear there's a supervisory role going up? You should definitely apply. I'll put an app in your mailbox, okay?"

I nod, my face red with happiness.

"By the way, you've got a medical assessment today, sucker!" Melissa calls from the other side of the room, pissed off that she's missing out on the attention.

Ah, shit.

Belinda nods at me. "The medical is waiting for you in the infirmary," she says. "But you'll be fine," she lies.

•

I go down to the ground floor and flick my wrist against the security scanner and enter the infirmary. As I walk in, I can see my data flash up on the large screen. There's a tall, thin medical who looks up at the SATISFACTORY on the screen and then turns and smiles at me.

"Full physical today, Will," he says.

•

I'm standing in front of the mirror for my medical assessment, dressed only in my old gray underpants. I hate this part the most. I hate people looking at my body. It's unreasonably thin and weird—my ribs stick out, there's no hair on my chest, there are bruises from the Crystal, and my stomach is hollow. My head looks huge above my skinny neck. My hair is shaved close to the skin—they make all Westie males do it. I've never managed the slightest shadow of a mustache, let alone a beard, so my cheekbones jut out, and so do my ears and chin. Then there's the new softness around my hips, stomach and chest—the Crystal will take a couple of days to kick in. Is it just me who can see it? I watch the medical closely, waiting for his face to change, but he's completely deadpan.

The medical presses down my spine, making notes, then presses the muscles along my inner thighs. I suck in my breath as he gets close to my underpants. I've heard they sometimes make you take your pants off so they can examine *everything*, but this has never happened to me. I've also heard that some medicals are straight-out pervs. Sometimes they're even Gray Corps affiliates who might recognize you from the Gray Zone and know that they can do whatever they want because you're scared they'll rat you out. His hands are cold.

"Okay, you can get dressed," he says, and I grab my clothes.

He's clicking through my data on the screen. Medicals have the same powers as CSOs—they can stick you in the Circle for rehab or send you to the Rator.

"You're still very underweight, Will," he says. "Have you been sticking to that meal plan you were assigned at your last medical?"

"Yes, sir," I lie. The truth is that Ma and I can't afford any of the food on that list. Besides, it'd be a waste—either the Crystal or the withdrawal makes me throw up most days.

"And you bought the vitamins the medical recommended last time?"

"Yes, sir," I lie.

"Are you taking any medication other than the vitamins we assigned you?"

"No, sir," I lie.

He looks up then. It's the first time he's really looked at me. His eyes are bright. He obviously isn't a moron. Does he *know*? I feel a spike of nausea. I'm paranoid everyone *knows*. It's exhausting. If he knows, then anything could happen—he could code me directly from his computer. And that would be it—the Rator van would be on its way. He sits there and watches me carefully. Then he says, "Physically, Will, you're barely hover- ing on satisfactory—you're well below average. I see from your motion studies report that you're maintaining a good output at the plant, but you're not going to be able to keep up long-term unless you build yourself up."

"I understand, sir." I'm trying to read his expression. I still can't tell whether he knows or not. I still can't tell what's going to happen.

He looks at me a long time. His eyes, I realize, are kind. Then he nods, "Okay, Will. You can go."

I nod and leave the room as slowly as I can force myself to. As soon as I'm outside in the break yard, I kneel on the ground and vomit violently onto the concrete.

.   •

I begin to stand up, still dizzy, and am about to put my mask on when the door bangs open and a CSO runs out and yells, "Lockdown!"

Shit, shit, shit, shit.

I throw myself on the floor. The medical's worked it out— he's sent the CSOs after me. My heart slams against my chest as I wait for the Taser to pierce my side.

Nothing happens. I look around. When I first came outside, I clocked a group of guys smoking and laughing on the other side of the yard, and they're all flat on the ground too. They're quiet and still, and I can feel their panic from where I'm lying. I mean, who here isn't doing something a bit illegal? Or *very* illegal, as the case may be. My heart banging, I slowly turn my head toward the CSO and see that he's walking *away* from me—away from the other guys as well—and that his focus is beyond the barbed wire fence that surrounds the plant.

It's got nothing to do with us.

The CSO walks back to us and adjusts his crotch. God, I hate CSOs. Then he tells us to get up—stand in place, hands behind our backs. "Afternoon, guys. I'm Corporate Security Officer H. This is a Code twelve-oh-five and you're all instructed to stay here until I tell you otherwise. At ease."

Everyone relaxes and starts to chat again as they realize he's not going to search us.

I look beyond the wire fence that surrounds the desal plant. There's a line of small girls on the other side of the street, wearing long, white dresses and blue sun hats, which match their blue face masks. One of them turns and looks at us. She's twelve or thirteen years old. She has a little puffy face and washed-out, creepy eyes—and I can see the dark curling brand down her cheek above the top of her mask. *Breeder*. It must be the hormones they give them, because when they're breeding, they all look the same—their faces get bloated and sleepy. This kid is heavily pregnant—seven, eight months—and she's holding her hands protectively across her hard, ballooning abdomen.

She sees me watching. I wave at her, and she screws up her face and gives me the finger. Then she turns to the kid next to her and whispers something, and the second kid looks at me too, and they laugh. Now their faces seem old—much, much older than the kids they are. There are around twenty Breeders, and they're all at late stages of pregnancy. They've just gotten out of a bright-red bus and are lining up at the end of a canal that opens out to the ocean. Even though the ocean is beyond the wall, there's a strip of dirty sand inside the zone, and from there you can see the gray waves through the electrified fencing. The Breeders are carrying lunch boxes and there's an old Shadow at the front of the line handing out plastic buckets and spades and balls—the kinds of toys you'd give much younger kids. It's a field trip. They've been brought here so they can take a look at the sea, chemical fires and all, then play on the petrol-licked sand, like real little kids—or as their Watchers imagine real little kids did, or would, in some theoretical and faraway world.

Then the whining starts. "Why do we have to look at Breeders? We pay our units like everyone else," a guy next to me says. His face is covered in zits—and his face is twisted in disgust. This sets off everyone else.

"It's gross."

"Foul."

"They shouldn't be allowed out in daylight."

I think of Alex then and I feel a knot in my stomach, but I don't say anything. And I especially don't point out that every guy here has a mother who was once a Breeder. Every Westie has to pay their dues to the Corp and for Breeders, there's only one way to do that.

I get these images in my head of Alex, pregnant. I try to stop them—it makes me want to vom just thinking about it— but they come anyway. To get that scar on her face, Alex must have been in the Incubator, and that means she's probably had at least one Corporation kid. Say Alex is fifteen—she could have had two or three kids already. After all, she doesn't have a Med tattoo, so she wasn't discharged for infertility.

Then there's the sound of shouting and banging. And sirens. Another CSO runs out into the break yard, a bleeding scratch down his face. "We need you out there!" he calls out to Officer H. "Those fucking Shadow bitches are coming up the street and they've gone crazy!"

"Shit," Officer H says, and follows him, and we wait about ten seconds until we run over to the perimeter fence to take a look. Five riot vans pull up in front of the plant and CSOs pour out in riot gear, carrying shields, masks, and batons. One group directs the little Breeders back onto the red bus. The other riot groups—shields up, batons ready—surge toward a large crowd coming from the other direction.

It's a crowd of Shadows, the red tattoo bright over the curling embryo brand on their cheeks. They're carrying placards and chanting.

"Down with the Breeder Laws! Down with the Corp!"

"Long Live the Response!"

I can't stop myself glancing at the other guys, who are looking at each other as well. The Response. You're not allowed to say the name aloud. I've heard all the stories about this underground resistance movement, of course. But nobody knows whether it really exists. And to be honest, it never occurred to me it could involve *Shadows*.

A Shadow at the front screams, "The Breeder Laws breach our human rights!" She's older than the others—maybe fifty years old, and she's wearing a knitted rainbow hat. She has sharp, intelligent eyes.

Human rights? Human rights are illegal.

The CSO phalanx reaches her, along with the tear gas. An officer smashes her to the ground and kicks her. Then he breaks her sign over his knee and grinds it into the asphalt. His face is red and full of rage and disgust. Her face is bleeding but her expression is impassive; her eyes stare out calmly.

The other CSOs rush forward on foot and start attacking the crowd, beating them hard with their batons, and tasing the Shadows once they hit the ground. The Shadows are all unarmed—their faces pale and still—but the officers are now firing rubber bullets as well as tear gas at them. They kick and punch the Shadows, smash their placards, turn their handbags and satchels upside down and scatter the contents.

We all go very quiet as we watch the older Shadow being cuffed and dragged into one of the vans, now unconscious, her right eye purple and half-shut, her knitted rainbow hat still on her head. Another, much younger Shadow is dragged behind her. She's got the red tattoo on her face and she's screaming, "The Response will get retribution from you all!" The officer who's dragging her away is tight-mouthed, his eyes glazed; he couldn't give a shit.

We watch the young Shadow being pushed into the back of the riot van. She's still screaming, "Don't you ever leave a person alone? When will you leave me alone?" and then the door is slammed and the siren starts and the van drives off.

The red bus starts to slowly back away from the canal, the little Breeders' faces pushed against the windows. I see the one who gave me the finger: she's watching a Shadow on the ground who's being kicked, again and again, even though it's clear she's been knocked unconscious. The Shadow's backpack has split open and bright red pamphlets are blowing down the street.

Officer H. is dragging a Shadow with long brown hair into another van. She's fighting him, punching his legs, and when she twists around to bite his hand, he hits her, right in the face. When her head falls backward, I see it's the Book Shadow. She's out cold, and he lifts her onto the floor of the van, and then shoves her feet in so hard it looks like he must be breaking them, and then he slams the door and spits on the ground.

Some of the Shadows are running away, their signs abandoned on the street. The CSOs go after them—some on foot, some slowly in their vans, jeering at them to run harder. I watch as every single Shadow is caught, cuffed, and thrown in the back of the windowless vans.

Then the vans pull out and drive away in a convoy. Behind them are the bags, signs, and pamphlets. Pools of blood and clumps of hair. One of the vans stops and an officer gets out, picks up each bag and takes wallets, purses, and IDs, then dumps the bags back onto the ground.

Then they're gone. The street's quiet, the clouds of tear gas are clearing. We are all still standing there. One of the guys, the one with the zits, starts to speak; changes his mind.

"Come on," someone says, and it's like we've come out of a long sleep. Then a few of us—me included—remember our need to smoke. We huddle together and someone takes out a pack of cigarettes. I light up. Then Lewis, a guy I've known for a couple of years, blurts out, "Well. It's good that they're cleaning up the streets—hopefully those vans will head straight to the Rator."

I feel a chill down my spine. "That's a bit harsh, Lewis."

He shrugs. "C'mon. You're not going to stick up for Shadow trash, are you? How are we meant to claw our way out of Zone F with them breaking the Laws, dragging us down?"

I see the Book Shadow, and Alex, in my mind. Before I can stop myself, I lurch forward and throw a punch at Lewis, and then they're all on me.

The CSOs are on top of us, dragging us apart. We're lined up, wrists out, screens up, and two officers go up and down the line, inspecting us. The biggest one stops when he gets to me and roughly grabs my hand, then swipes my chip with his scanner. I see on the little screen sewn into my wrist that he's taken eighty units. Then he takes forty units from Lewis, who's shaking.

Security make us stand there for another thirty minutes, holding our hands out until our arms ache, knowing full well that we'll be deducted further lateness units when we go back to our workstations. Sadistic assholes.

"Dismissed," one of them says finally, and we walk quickly toward the door, everyone looking daggers at me.

"What the fuck, Will?" Lewis says, as we walk back into the building.

I don't answer.

"Will?" he says. "Aren't you going to say anything?" He's pissed.

I shrug him off and jog into the building.

•

A few mornings after the Responder protest, my heart racing, I go down the street in the Old Town to the Book Shadow's shop and hold my wrist to the security scanner, frightened about what I will find, but unable to stay away. The scanner beeps red and won't let me in. I knock on the door and there's no answer. I walk around the building looking for open windows and everything is shut up and the blinds are all closed. I knock again and the door of a neighboring shop—"Tailor"—opens and a small, older man peers out. I want to say something, to ask about the Book Shadow, but then I turn and leave without saying anything.

The following week, I walk down the same street and stop: the whole building has been fire-bombed. There are barriers up and down the street and I can't get within one hundred feet of the door.

•

Alex and I meet every Wednesday morning after our Gray Corps work at the revolting diner that's just outside the Gray Zone security checkpoint. It's a twenty-four-hour diner, so Gray Corps affiliates and CSOs and runners and all the other night people are here, and it's generally acknowledged to be neutral ground, unless someone does something particularly stupid. I always get there first and have to wait for Alex. Rob drops me off at the diner around 4:30 a.m., and Alex comes in an hour later. I don't know what Alex does all night with her Gray Corps affiliate—she still won't say.

I'm happy with the steady supply of Crystal 10 and with the bonus units. Every Tuesday night, I meet Rob at the Wall. Every Tuesday night, I spend two hours at the Gate, on the edge of the badlands, trading gold for Breeders. Every Wednesday morning, I mentally review the following facts: I take Breeders from their families, sometimes by force, and give their parents a little bit of gold in return; I carry sometimes-screaming Breeders back across the Gate; I help drug the Breeders; I help put Breeders in the back of a gold SUV and hope they don't suffocate before they get to the Incubator; once at the Incubator, they're unloaded by someone else. I don't know exactly what happens to them, but I have a pretty good idea. I take all those facts and I put them in a black box inside my mind, and I don't open that box until the following Tuesday evening, when I say goodbye to Ma and head down to the Wall again.

Alex and I have a coffee before I go home to shower, and then go work at the desal plant, and before Alex goes home to do whatever it is she does during the day—she won't tell me about that either, except that she has to stay inside and out of sight. Alex and I always sit in a booth at the back. The diner predates the End Times—it's one of those buildings that for arbitrary reasons remained standing while the others on the block were razed to the ground in the burning and bombing and terror. The seats are covered in faded red vinyl and the tables in light-blue laminate. Alex takes out a tissue from her pocket and slowly runs it along the table. The diner isn't a nice place or anything. The owners must make a pile of units off us and the Gray Corps, but you can tell they hate serving all of us. Things that get broken stay broken, and several of the seats' vinyl backs have been torn or ripped; there are cracks along the surface of most of the tables. Ours is an exception, which is one reason we like it. They don't even bother cleaning the place properly, so there's a film of grease on the floor, and blotches of mustard and cream on the surface of our table that Alex is painstakingly wiping off.

Alex's mother is a serious Mood who's on buckets of medication and can't work, so Alex's income from the Wall is all they've got. Alex told me that her mother was kidnapped by some Corp explorers from a Western city a few years before Alex was born. When I say that's impossible, that the land was burned out a long time ago, that there are no Western cities, Alex raises an eyebrow and says, "Do you honestly believe everything the Corp tells you?" But when I ask her to explain, she won't. And she won't tell me about how she ended up in the Incubator, or, more importantly, how she got out. I still don't get how Alex can go around as a Breeder without getting caught—there are seriously so many people everywhere, even in the Gray Zone, who would rat you out for a few units. The diner is full of Wall Kids like her, and she's grown up with some of them but the kids her age are guys—sooner or later, all the Breeders are sent to the Incubator, even here in the Gray Zone. Alex must be protected by someone. She seems to have a source for scan patches whenever she wants to leave the Gray Zone—it's the only way she can move between zones. You inject them into your wrist to fool the scanners into thinking you have access, and then they dissolve within twenty-four hours.

We like spending time together . . . I think. Well, *I* like spending time with *her*, but she also makes me nervous. I get scared I might accidentally touch her. And if I think about her too much, about her being a Breeder—it still makes me feel strange. I handle Breeders all night at the Wall, but that's a truth for the black box. Although Alex is a Breeder, she's also like nobody I've ever met before. She knows things—she knows much more than I do. She knows things beyond what the Corp tells us.

Alex has never been to school and she says she'll never do proper work for units within the Corp, ever. She'll live her life in the Gray Zone. She's fascinated by how I go about my days—the desal plant, school, the monthly tallying of units. She's fascinated by my recounting of the End Times, which she says are all lies. Her eyes sparkle when she says this, and I can't tell whether she's joking or not.

"Go on, recite me some history!" Alex says now, smiling. She roared with laughter when I first told her that our history lessons were taught through *The Horrors of the End Times*. She thinks it's hilarious that I've seen it six hundred times and can recite the whole two hours verbatim.

I shrug. *"After the End Times, over a billion people starved to death. The survivors decided that kind of violence and poverty and starvation was never going to happen again, and that the only way forward was to make every decision based on creating economic prosperity. The Corporation drew a line around the settlement, and then they built the Wall on that boundary. They put barbed wire outside the wall, and cameras and guards. They sent the machines out to monitor the perimeter . . ."*

"More! I want more history!" Alex shouts, laughing, and I continue.

"There are over five million people in the Corporation, and it's big enough to sustain its own economy. Nobody goes in or out. Neither do any goods or trading. We don't want foreign materials disturbing the balance of our delicate economy. The Corporation decided long ago to remove the tyranny of government to avoid repeating the End Times, which was caused by government interference. The best decision our original settlers made was to allow the market to take care of itself. Our Corporation leaders are a conglomeration of CEOs from the biggest companies. They're the ones who know how policy is going to influence business, and the quality of our daily lives. Efficiency is of the utmost importance."

By now Alex has stopped laughing and is shaking her head at me. I don't say anything more, even though I know the next part by heart too: *The Corporation writes the Laws, which include strict rules about who is allowed to reproduce, and how. The Laws manage every life, and determine who is allowed to Breed, and how. Breeders are a special category . . ."* I don't want to say *Breeder* in front of Alex.

I can tell that Alex thinks I'm an idiot. I can see the acid sea from where I work at the plant, but other than that, I have to admit that I have no proof that what the Corp tells us is true. I asked Ma about it, after the Shadow protest at the desal plant, and she asked me who I'd been talking to.

"Nobody!" I told her. "Who do you think? The *Response*?" Ma went white and looked around. She made a sign at me—a knife across her throat. *Cut it out*. She wasn't being paranoid. Our house could be bugged by the Corp.

"What's it like, living there?" Alex asks. Even though she lives in the Gray Zone, it's an off-the-grid economy that's in many ways outside the Corporation.

I shrug. It's hard to explain the only thing you've ever known. I don't tell Alex that everyone in Zone F feels almost as sorry for the Wall Kids as for the Westies beyond the Wall. And I can't tell her the truth of everything I've done, and everything I am. So I start by telling Alex some stories about when I was a kid.

Once, I tell her, my class went on a school excursion to a film set located in Zone C, called Horrors of the End Times World, where parts of the documentary were actually made. The whole set has been preserved, so that our history can be told for generations to come.

They've hired all the nonfamous actors from the documentary, and they reenact key scenes of misery and desperation from the film, showing how people really lived and died during the End Times. On one set, there's a housewife with boils all over her face, crying that she has no food to give her baby, who has the plague anyway. On another set, a farmer sets fire to his crop because it's covered in maggots. There's the scene of the Traitor on the Gibbet, who has a spear shoved through the bottom of his feet and through his body, as an example to others. Best of all, I tell Alex, is the set of the Cannibalism of the

Innocents, where an intake of Westies was sacrificed for Corp food after a bad harvest.

Alex grins at me. "And you totally believe that's the truth? Like, that it's *history*?"

I sigh, annoyed. "Look. I know my Zone F education is shit. Okay?"

Alex shakes her head. "Don't get pissed at me."

"I'm not," I lie. "It's just . . . How about you tell me about what it was like growing up here, in the Gray Zone?"

She smiles.

"Well?"

"Well . . . a lot of parents try to preserve Westie culture, which is nice."

"Like what?"

"In the winter we always have Bonfire Night."

"Okay."

"Yeah. It's from old Westie history. Once, the Westie common people murdered a corrupt king by burning him alive."

I laugh. That sounds really "nice."

"So every kid makes a king . . ."

"You make a king?"

"Out of some old pants and a shirt and stuff. You fill him up with paper. And you stick a crown on him. And then you put him on your shoulders and take him door-to-door, saying 'a dollar for the king?'"

"You're collecting money for—the elderly and the sick?"

She snorts. "No, for ourselves!"

"Okay. Very *nice*. Then what?"

"Well, then we build a big fire at the reservoir. We put all the kings on top of the fire and burn them. You know, just blow them all up. Then there are fireworks . . ."

"Sounds . . . interesting." Alex and her childhood sure are a trip.

"It's great! The same night, all the little kids leave their pillow-cases outside with a box of matches on top. If our pillowcases aren't filled up with stuff, the legend is that we'll light a match and burn the zone down. So in the morning, we find presents, gold pieces, new clothes and shoes."

"It's filled up by, like, a magic fairy, or something?"

"Nope. By the Gray Corps affiliates. Who are usually our fathers . . . Obviously."

"I see."

Alex is embarrassed. She gulps her last bit of coffee and then says, "Hey! Do you wanna go on a trip to Zone C with me?"

I almost spit out my coffee. "Come on!" Alex says. "I have injectables," she whispers. "They cost me a packet."

"There's *no way*," I tell her. "Have you heard about the latest Breeder rapes?"

She sighs. "No need to tell me. Nothing surprises me about humans. *Nothing*."

I still tell her about the latest murder of a Breeder, in the canal down past one of the tech schools. "Raped and murdered by a bunch of thirteen-year-old Wasters," I say. "Never mind the CSOs taking you to the Rator, Alex, there are kids out there who will kill you on sight."

"The depths of human depravity, Will. Distract me. Tell me more about your dream job."

"Shut up!" I say, smiling. She's been teasing me about it relentlessly.

"No, I mean it. I'm sorry I made fun of you before. I want to hear more."

I tell her again about how the desal plant has a supervision position opening up, and because I've painstakingly gained extra units from my electronics work, I'm allowed to take a promotion test for a potential level up. It would put me on track for an early transfer to Zone E.

"That's exciting!" Alex says.

"Yeah," I tell her. "If I get it, they might even let me put down a deposit for a car."

Her eyes are glittering. She's totally making fun of me.

"Shut up!" I tell her. I punch her lightly on her shoulder. She hits me back.

"So, what, they just suddenly opened up this supervisor job?" she says, pretending she's interested.

"Well, they did an audit day at the plant," I say.

"And?"

"They have spots open because they got rid of ten percent of the staff." I don't tell her that we call these *Rator Days*. We never know when they're coming. You just walk into the plant one morning and a bunch of windowless vans are lined up in the parking lot. At the end of the workday, those vans will be taking the bottom 10 percent to the Rator. Sometimes, you can tell it's actually more than 10 percent—that's if the Corp is freaking out about excess Westies not contributing enough units. They just don't need that many male bodies.

"Don't you worry that one day that will be *you*?" Alex asks.

I shrug. "Not really. I'm always at least average in my tests and stuff."

"And ten percent of your friends disappear and that doesn't, like, worry you?" she asks, alarmed.

"They're not my friends. I just work with them. And it

means less competition for units." I grin at her. I'm kidding. Kind of.

We look at each other. And because I feel embarrassed, a little put on the spot, I blurt out, "How did you get out of the Incubator anyway? Did someone buy you out?"

She looks down, her face growing red. I regret asking her instantly.

"I'm sorry . . ." I say. "I didn't mean . . ."

"It was the Response," she says.

I look around, panicked. You just don't say that word aloud in a public space. At all. Ever. According to the Corps, the Response doesn't exist. But if you say it does, and they hear you . . .

"Hey . . . It's my birthday today," I say quietly to distract her. "Though not officially."

"Officially, nobody here has a birthday. Don't worry."

She reaches for my hand and our fingers touch and I flinch. I try to hide it but it's hopeless. I can tell she's confused by my reaction and I feel a ball of shame and anger in my stomach. I wish everything weren't so hard. I wish I weren't such a coward.

"I don't get it," she says.

"What?"

"Well, you want to grow up and be a profesh and get a house and a wife, yeah?"

"Yeah."

"But you can't even touch my *finger*." She cracks a smile.

I shudder, and she laughs.

"*Finger!*" She laughs again.

"Shut up!"

"You should see your face right now!"

I look away. She's still laughing. "But *why*, Will . . . ?"

"I dunno," I tell her, honestly. I feel such big, conflicting things when I'm around Alex. "For a start, Breeders *literally* belong to the Corp," I blurt out.

I see her face.

"I don't mean you," I say quickly.

"Yes, you do," she says. "But it's okay. Just tell me: How does that change, exactly, when Breeders become Shadows?"

"Well, according to Corp law . . ."

She rolls her eyes at me. "Again, you don't have to believe every single thing the Corp tells you."

"What do you mean?"

"Well, for a start, there's no such thing as Breeders and Shadows," she says. "They're just words the Corp made up. We're *women* and *girls* or just, you know, *people*."

I don't say anything.

"For another thing, the Response is real," she says, too loudly. She sees the panic in my face and she laughs. Then she takes my hand again, and this time I let her. I hold her hand back. "Happy birthday, Will."

"Thanks."

She looks at me carefully. Too carefully. Like she can see who I really am.

•

When I get home, Cranky is loose in the front yard and I can hear Ma inside the house, shouting and swearing in Westie.

Ma only drinks once a year, on my birthday, which is of course also the anniversary of my mother's suicide.

The front door swings open and Ma is standing there,

throwing handfuls of gold pieces down our front stairs. The gold I got from Breeder running.

"Blood money!" Ma shouts, as I run around collecting the pieces as they bounce off the ground in the dawn light, hoping nobody can see us. I put them carefully in my pocket because Ma will want them later, when she's calmed down and practical again. Ma watches me. Then she pushes past me and goes to Cranky and feeds him some herbs from her pockets.

"The Corporation are fucking shits!" Ma shouts.

"Ma, shhhh," I say, looking around. "Come on inside."

Ma begins to cry. She never cries. I put my arms around her and take her upstairs. I help her onto her bed and take her shoes off and tuck her in. She's still crying. I put the blankets around her chin.

"It's okay, Ma. It really is," I tell her.

"They are *shits*, Will. We work our guts out so they can drink champagne. Don't give them anything extra, okay? No supervision work." I hadn't told her that I was applying for the promotion because I knew she wouldn't approve and I wanted to get it before I told her, but Ma has friends all over the plant and it was only a matter of time before she found out.

"Okay, Ma."

"It's important you don't stand out for any reason."

"Okay, Ma."

"Promise me, Will. People don't like supervisors. There'll be too much talk. Promise me."

"I promise, Ma."

"And Will, stop talking about having a wife and kids. You know that can't happen. Stop standing out. Just survive, Will, and try to be happy. That's all there is. I know it isn't easy. But it matters. I want you to find something that makes you happy. Promise me?"

"Okay."

"Just survive. Do the minimum for the Corp. And live your life. Okay?"

"Okay, Ma."

•

Later that morning, I tell Belinda to withdraw my supervisor's application because most of the applicants are a couple years older with more experience and besides, I'm worried about the twenty unit fee. Belinda is disappointed, and Melissa looks victorious—I wasn't one of the guys she was rooting for, so she was totally sour about me applying. A few days later, Melissa organizes a cake for the guy who ends up getting the position, a dude from Floor 8 of the desal—Evan. At the congratulatory celebration, Evan shows me a picture of the car he's put a deposit on. He's already ordered a catalogue of up-and-coming Shadows from the Incubator and he's thinking about taking the next step of opening a thirty-year lay-by plan.

•

One Tuesday evening, Rob arranges to pick me up just inside the Gray Zone at sunset. He's tense, and when I ask him about my next job, and why we're starting so early, he just says, sarcastically, "Corporate work." Instead of heading east, farther into the Gray Zone, we drive north, toward the center of the Corp.

Rob is a Corp lawyer. Some Gray Corps affiliates start out as

Westies like me, then work their way up the Breeder running or drug smuggling chain and climb the Gray Corps ranks that way. But Rob is true Corp, born and bred. I don't know why someone born into the Corp would take a bad turn—sure, he makes loads of money as a Gray Corps affiliate, but he has a lot to lose. Maybe he has a drug habit? Maybe he enjoys the thrill of life in the Gray Zone? Maybe he's a naturally crooked guy who couldn't walk a straight line if he tried?

Rob drives onto a ramp and I realize we're on the exclusive Corp freeway that cuts across all the zones—the module at the top of his car windscreen beeps happily as we pass each checkpoint scanner. I'm dying to see inside the other zones but the freeway is bordered by fifteen-foot walls, so I see nothing.

Then we go down another ramp and his car slows in front of a physical checkpoint marked ZONE B. It's a large sandstone gate with about twenty armed CSOs holding semiautomatics, along with the usual Tasers. One steps forward as Rob rolls down his window and holds out his wrist for scanning.

Rob says, "We're here for Case Three-Eight-Two-Seven," and the guard nods.

"We're going to send an escort with you to the magistrate's court."

We roll through the gates with two CSO motorbikes in front of us and two following.

I put my mask on and roll down the car window because I've never been in Zone B before. I've heard about it from Ma, but she doesn't remember much from her visits over fifteen years ago. As we drive along the main street, I see how clean it is, and how streamlined: the sleek, high-rise buildings; the tree-lined streets. I take as much of it in as I can: the astounding variety of beautiful clothes that people are wearing; the bright colors of the shopfronts and restaurants.

We follow the CSO bikes down a spiraling driveway—down, down into the parking garage of a high-rise building.

Rob is very anxious. I've never seen him like this.

"Don't say a thing," he tells me. "Just follow my lead."

The CSOs lead us to an elevator, which takes us into an enclosed room—a courtroom with insignia and expensive furniture and a stenographer in the corner, ready to take notes. An older man in a uniform is sitting on the edge of a large bench at the front of the room. He comes over and tells us he's a court officer and that he needs our names and details. Rob writes some lies on a form. During the next half hour, more senior Gray Corps affiliates, like Rob, file in. I'm the only Wall Kid, of course, but nobody seems bothered by me being here.

Then we're asked to sit, and the court officer lifts a hammer and lets it fall.

"*All rise for Irregular Hearing No. Three-Eight-Two-Seven of Year 352 of the Corporation.*"

We stand again as the door at the front of the court, to the left of the long bench, opens and another old man comes in, wearing black robes.

The old man sits in a golden chair behind the front tables.

The old man—the magistrate—starts talking. He speaks quickly, in a bored tone. It's 7:40 p.m. on a Tuesday night and he's probably meant to be at a fancy dinner in Zone A. The stenographer taps away.

"This is an Extraordinary Trial of sixty-eight Shadows based on events that took place earlier today."

What events? I look at Rob, but he doesn't meet my gaze.

"Given the urgency of the matter," the magistrate continues, "I am applying Regulation Thirty-Five of the Laws, which suspends the Rule of Law. Accordingly, I am going to provide a brief account of facts and charges, and then a verdict. Then I will move immediately to sentencing. For the sake of brevity and to prevent further disturbances, I will leave the defendants in the holding cells until the time of sentencing. Since these defendants fall under the Special Laws, they are not entitled to representation or a voice in this court. Stenographer, I'll begin by setting out the names, ages, and occupations of the sixty-eight Shadows who have been charged."

The stenographer nods and the magistrate begins: "Cynthia Watts, thirty-five, clerk; Rachel Garner, thirty-eight, accounting officer; Stacey Nesles, forty-two, teacher; Ellen Hooper, forty-one, paralegal . . ."

It takes a long time to read through all the defendants. It sounds like they're Zone B profesh Shadows. To be Zone B profesh, Shadows must have come out of the Incubator with an excellent fertility record *and* still be physically and psychologically strong enough to take up a profesh position. I can't think why a legal assistant, publisher, or scientific officer would give up a life in Zone B, so hard-won, to commit crimes against the Corp.

Then the magistrate describes the acts: "On this day, the defendants assembled at Corporation Square in Zone B. They accosted passersby and tried to engage them, and then set off an incendiary device, killing thirty-five innocent Zone B citizens, eleven CSOs, and three members of their own group."

I look at Rob, who turns away from me. There was an explosion in Zone B? How come we didn't hear about it? I'm still thinking about this when the court officer brings a black square of fabric to the magistrate, and the magistrate puts it on his head.

"The charges of mutiny, unrest, and murder have been made out," the magistrate says. "I find the defendants guilty on all charges. Officer, could you bring the defendants up from the holding cells for the reading of the sentences?"

The court officer goes out the door that's behind the magistrate and we hear murmured voices and shuffling feet. Then a hatch opens right in the center of the courtroom floor, and a procession of Shadows emerges, climbing up a circular staircase from the holding cell beneath the ground. As they emerge, the magistrate begins to read the sentences.

"Cynthia Watts, thirty-five, clerk, I find you guilty of the charges so laid. You are sentenced to death."

Cynthia Watts raises her right fist and shouts, "Long live the Breeder Response!"

The court officer bangs his hammer, but she ignores him and keeps chanting.

"Rachel Garner, thirty-eight, accounting officer, I find you guilty of the charges so laid. You are sentenced to death."

Rachel raises her right fist and also shouts, "Long live the Response!"

"Stacey Nesles, forty-two, teacher, I find you guilty of charges so laid. You are sentenced to death."

Stacey is also shouting, and there's more shouting coming from the people behind her. I can't hear the magistrate, who's looking desperately at the officer, who can't do anything. So the magistrate just keeps reading through all sixty-eight sentences, even though nobody can hear him, as quickly as he can. Then he clears his throat and nods to the court officer, who opens the little door and the magistrate scurries away.

Rob and the other Gray Corps affiliates step forward as

security corrals all sixty-eight Shadows into small groups. Each Shadow has a CSO holding her wrist. Rob motions for me to come help him. We lead six of the CSOs with their Shadows, still shouting, out of the courtroom and down the elevator into the bowels of the garage. Then we take them to Rob's car and one by one, load them in the back. I'm conscious of how fragile their spines feel as I push them—as gently as possible—into the back of the SUV. They're slow and careful with each other, murmuring directions, so as not to hurt each other as they climb up. The last in the line is Stacey. Unlike the others, she doesn't look down with care as she steps up into the back of the SUV but looks at me, defiant. When I step near to help her, she throws her arm back to strike me. But she misses, and Rob slams past me and grabs Stacey, then roughly shoves her inside and slams the door shut.

We drive to another security checkpoint. When we pull up, some of the Shadows start to wail and I look out the window at the sign across the gate. *The Incinerator.* Otherwise known as the Rator. It's about sixty feet tall and out the top plumes black smoke. This is where you go if your units are irretrievably in debt, or you're sentenced to death by law, or the Corp otherwise wants to get rid of you. Rob hands the court documents through the window and we're waved through.

We unload the Shadows so they can be processed into the Rator individually. Stacey turns to me again, her eyes still bright with rage.

She looks me in the eye. "Traitor!" she shouts, and spits in my face. I wipe the spit off and get back in the car.

Rob and I are silent as he drives away, and when we're back on the Corp freeway, he says, "I wanted you to see what happens to members of the Response, Will."

His eyes meet mine in the rearview mirror. What has he heard? "The Response killed fifty people through some stunt today, and now you just saw sixty-eight members get executed. None of it made any difference whatsoever to the Corp. It's totally futile. I'd hate you to just throw yourself away like that. Do you understand?"

I nod.

"Obviously, you can't mention this to anyone. You won't see it appearing in any news feeds either."

I close my eyes, feeling heartsick with myself. I'm shaking, and I can see Stacey's eyes in front of me: *Traitor.* She's right—I just handed them over without hesitation. I tell myself to put those thoughts in the black box. I tell myself I need to rest during the hour's drive back to the Gray Zone, because soon my shift of Breeder running will start.

•

I'm still shaking hours later, after I've finished Breeder running and am dropped off at the diner. I'm still shaking thirty minutes after *that*, when Alex comes in and I'm drinking my seventh cup of coffee. She must be able to tell, because she comes and sits next to me, rather than opposite. I'm conscious of her leg touching my leg, of her hesitating about whether to put her arm around me. I'm scared—I don't want to touch her again, and yet I do.

When Alex asks me what's wrong, I can't tell her about the Breeder running, I can't tell her about the Shadows and the court case, so I just shake my head. Then she says, "It's okay. You don't have to tell me," and she takes my hand. Her hand feels very warm and very good. She can never know that I'm a runner.

I order food—screw the expense. I don't have the strength to be cheap. Our waiter, who's also the owner's son, bangs the plate down in front of me, resentment oozing out of him—everyone assumes that us Wall Kids are diseased, criminal, and violent Moods—so I make a sudden move for the ketchup and watch him flinch. He glares at me and humphs off, and I find that I'm staring at the ugliest plate of eggs I've ever seen. On the edge of the plate are two pieces of toast that look like they've been dragged along the filthy floor and then left under a running tap. I don't care; I'm starving

"Just looking at your breakfast makes me want to kill myself," Alex says cheerfully. She's ordered her usual black coffee, and it's arrived in a mug about the size of her big, weird hat.

"Don't look at it, then," I tell her, and shove in a forkful. Alex sips her coffee. As I shovel more food into my mouth, I notice someone is watching us: a Gray Corps affiliate at the next table is openly staring at Alex. With those eyes, Alex always gets a lot of attention. But the paranoid part of me can't help but wonder if he can see the tip of her Breeder mark below her hat. *I* can't see her mark, but I reach over and pull her hat down extra tight just in case.

"Hey." Alex says. Then I see Alex clock the Gray Corps guy staring at her, and I blurt out, "Where do you go with Mr. Gold-bags, anyway? I never see you down at the Wall. You're too little to fight. What does he make you do, anyway?"

Alex laughs, and I feel uneasy.

"What? What's so funny?"

"Mr. Goldbags isn't a 'he.' *She*'s a woman."

"A *woman*?" The word is strange in my mouth. Alex never uses the words *Breeder* and *Shadow*. Always girl and woman and person.

"Yeah, a woman," Alex says, drinking her coffee. I live in a world of boys and men. In the Before times, there would have been girls in my class, women in the streets. There aren't girls or women anywhere now—only Breeders and Shadows. But Alex doesn't see herself as a Breeder, she sees herself as a girl. An old-world concept. Alex sees the world differently and she doesn't care that the way she sees the world doesn't match up with the Corp's view. What would she think if she knew I was a Breeder runner? She would hate me with all her heart. I know Alex wouldn't be a runner for any reason—not even for her own life.

"You work for a Shadow who works for the Gray Corps?" I whisper to her. It doesn't make sense. Alex looks at me closely.

"No, not the Gray Corps," she says. "She's part of the Response."

Oh fuck. "How does a Shadow do Response work in the Gray Zone without getting taken down?" I ask. The Gray Zone belongs to the Gray Corps. They turn a blind eye to Alex and the other kids of Gray Corps affiliates, they'll even look after them, in their way—but I don't see why the Gray Corps would let the Response operate in the Gray Zone in plain sight.

Alex just shrugs and smiles.

"Hang on. *You're* not part of the Response, are you?" I ask, panic rising.

She stops smiling. She doesn't answer.

"Alex?" I say. "Don't you trust me?"

She shakes her head. "I can't tell you any more, Will."

"But . . ."

"In the meantime," Alex says, opening her hand, eyes glittering. "You up for it?"

In the palm of her hand are two pills. Her *Shadow* has given her some Jazz. For weeks now, Alex has been obsessed with me skipping work and taking Jazz with her, and then both of us heading into Zone C. *I've* been obsessed with not being sent to the Rator. Memo is one thing, but with Jazz . . . anything can happen to you on that stuff. She grins at me again and holds up her hand. Fighting with Alex is useless—it's better to let her talk up her plans and then say goodbye when I've finished my breakfast.

"*Please* let's go to Zone C today," Alex says. "We could go *shopping*." I laugh, because the thought of Alex bouncing around a shopping center is unreal. What the hell would she buy? I try to imagine her going into a fancy department store and buying . . . another fucking hat?

I don't say anything. I just eat my eggs and try to distract her with something I've actually been thinking about.

"Hey, you know how you said it's all lies about the . . . you know . . . the End Times and stuff," I look around to make sure nobody's listening, and Alex laughs at me. "Well, I've seen the burnt ocean from the desal plant. I've seen the burnt land from the top of the Wall. And I've seen all the Westies waiting outside the Wall. People aren't making that stuff up. So what do you mean?"

"Sure, there were End Times," Alex says. "And the badlands *are* terrible—but not all areas were hit as bad as ours was. The Corp has deliberately cut us off from those other places. There are rumors that other cities are trying to contact us and the Corp won't let them. The Corp's 'exploration' is actually about keeping us isolated. They're blowing up any bridges or communication lines that they can find."

"But *why*?"

Her exasperation takes me by surprise. "Because our Corp overlords have it great here! Their Zone A life is *amazing*. They have it all worked out. They don't need to trade. They don't need or want contact with other countries, other people. They can just live off us Westies."

I'm shaking my head. Alex and I sit still, glaring at each other.

"I don't know," I say. My voice sounds more pissed than I intended.

"Why are you arguing with me?"

"Well, why are you arguing with *me*?"

"Is it so incredible to you that the Corp would lie about our history, about what it's doing?"

"Well, no. But . . . but everything we do here is for all the zones. Not just Zone A. Westies benefit too."

"It's mainly for Zone A."

"But . . ."

"*C'mon*, Will," she says. "You're the one who asked. Why does talking about this make you so angry?"

I honestly don't know. All those times I had to recite that crap about the End Times in school—I mean, I knew I wasn't at a proper school, learning real things, like kids in Zone B or even Zone C. But I never thought they were actual lies. She shrugs. "Maybe let's not talk politics today. Do you know how long it's been since I've left the Gray Zone?"

She reaches into her pocket again and holds up two tiny syringes with large caps on them. "Scan patches!" she says, grinning. My stomach flips.

"Are you crazy? Hide them!" She laughs and puts her hands under the table.

"Come on, Will! With these patches, we're two humble sewerage plant workers, and today's our well-deserved day off. Party day. Don't you want to celebrate with me? We have *Zone C* access!" she says.

She's nuts. It's suicide. "What about your scar?" I ask.

She takes a compact out of her bag. "Concealer," she says. "Come with me."

She grabs my arm and her bag and we go to the bathroom, where Alex locks us in a stall. Then she flips open the compact and takes out a little brush, applying thick makeup to her face until one side is covered. She puts her hat on and pulls it down over the brand.

"Oh, come on, Alex."

"What?"

"That's—that's insanely risky."

"Risk is part of the fun."

"Shit."

She takes the cap off a syringe and expertly injects the inside of her wrist. Then she takes my wrist and I feel her warm hand as she tries to find the scanner chip under my skin. It would be fun, of course—we could run around and laugh at the crap posh people in the upper zones—and it would be a trip to hear Alex's opinion of things she hadn't seen, or hadn't seen in a long time. But all she'd need is one CSO to look at her a little too closely, and she'd be in for it. She's so used to the Gray Corps looking the other way, she's become deluded that a little makeup and a hat will do the trick outside the Gray Zone. I push her hand away.

"Come on, Will," she says.

I shake my head.

"If you come, I'll tell you about the Response. I mean, I know you're in love with the Corp but . . ." She grins at me.

She's still holding my hand. My heart is racing, and I'm going to be sick. I think of the line of Shadows being thrown into the Rator.

"No," I say. I pull my arm away fast and leave the stall. She follows me back to the table, frowning.

"It's not that I love the Corp . . ." I say, as quietly as I can. "It's just . . . I've seen the Response get smashed by the Corp. They don't stand a chance."

She looks at me carefully. "We're only getting started, Will. The Response is growing. Come with me today, and I'll tell you more about us." *Us.* I think of the protesters getting beaten. The slim spines of the women as I push them into the back of Rob's SUV. I'm finding it hard to breathe.

Then I notice the same large man who was looking at Alex before has moved places, and he's now sitting at the table next to us pretending to enjoy his entertainment plug. He's not a pervy Gray Corps affiliate after all—he's a CSO. Fuck. *Fuck.* He doesn't have a uniform or a badge, but it's clear to anyone with the slightest clue that he's security: a huge, stupid-eyed guy with massive arms and a mean mouth. They're fucking *every-where* now—the crackdown is real.

Something alerts Alex to him too and her face changes to fear. She freezes.

Ah, shit. "C'mon," I whisper. "Do it. Inject me. Let's go."

I can see her calming down. She smiles. "Really?"

"Yeah, yeah. Let's get out of here!" I pull her out of the booth and we go back to the bathroom and I feel a cold sting as she pushes the tiny syringe into my wrist and then she pushes a Jazz pill into my mouth and one into hers.

•

We put on our masks and run down to the main road and then out the gates of the Gray Zone. We keep running until we get to a bus stop and we jump onto an orange Transit-bound bus that's about to pull away from the curb. I scan my wrist against the scanner and it beeps and then I watch Alex push her wrist against it too and am relieved when it beeps her through. She laughs happily and I go down the aisle, dragging Alex behind me, holding her firmly by the hand. For a moment, I feel giddy with happiness. I'll lose one hundred units for missing my morning shift, but I'll make sure I'm back for the afternoon shift, and I'll tell them I was sick—I haven't had a sick day in three years. I get to spend a few hours clear with Alex. I feel a pang about Ma not seeing me come home from the Gray Zone before she goes to work, because she'll worry. But if I send her a message, it might be intercepted, and I can call her later from work. It's better if she thinks I've been held up at the Wall. Ma would worry much, *much* more if I told her I was "hanging out"—given that I live life as a forty-year-old, she would smell a rat.

Right now, I can't stand the thought of people touching me—but the bus is packed with men and boys, so I give up and just try to ignore the pressure and smells and sounds of all those bodies. A tall man pressing against me is clearly another CSO. Fuck. Again, there's no uniform or a badge—it's obvious though: a huge, well-nourished, stupid-eyed guy with expensive sunglasses.

I look around to see if he's already tracking anyone and notice there's a Shadow on the bus. She's in her late twenties, very thin, standing near the back door, with a foot-wide space around her—none of the men want to touch her. Her eyes are bright with pain. A Mood. She hasn't noticed the CSO—she's staring out the window, frowning and fretting as though she's lost something and is searching the pavement for it as we drive along. Still watching her, the CSO takes his phone out of his pocket and taps something into it. It looks like he's waiting for her to do something wrong, like committing an act of public nuisance—which technically could be something as small as talking to herself out loud, or wearing too much deodorant. CSOs tend to target Shadows for minor infractions much more than they target the rest of us. Or he might just hassle her for no ostensible reason at all, just because he can. I catch Alex's eye and she nods; she's clocked both the CSO and the Shadow. I look at the CSO again and he must feel my eyes on him because he gives me a good stare, which sends a shot of panic up my spine. He could ask to scan my ID, frisk me—hell, he could arrest me, no questions asked, and give me a cavity search if he wanted. CSOs have a right to detain you for as long as they want; Ma has drilled that into me since I could walk. He's still staring at me.

Then I feel a warmth flow up my body, from my toes to the top of my head and I no longer give a shit. It's the Jazz. Alex is grinning at me. It's as though something deep inside me drops out—there's a feeling that somehow, I don't have a pilot anymore. I'm thinking about Alex and the waking nightmare of my night with the Shadows and the Breeders and wishing I could just make something good happen. I watch myself from a distance as I take a step around the CSO, blocking his view of the Shadow at the door, and I look him straight in the face and say, "Excuse me?"

Someone nearby clears his throat: a middle-aged man dressed in a nice suit, who is gently shaking his head at me in warning.

I turn back to the officer. "Excuse me, do you know which stop I'd get off for Edgecombe Road?"

The man in the suit grabs my arm as though to steady me. The CSO pushes him away. "You stay out of this!" he snarls at the older man and then he says to me, "What exactly is your problem?" My heart's going mental and my brain is telling me that it would be much more sensible to walk out into the badlands if I want to destroy myself, rather than allow some CSO bastard to get his hands on me, but my brain is somehow not in control. I can see Alex whispering to the Shadow, who glances up, her face full of terror, and locks eyes with the CSO.

Around us there's one of those waves of freaking out, as each person takes a proper look at the CSO and realizes what he is—and they all scamper to the other end of the bus. Who knows how many Gray Corps and smugglers are traveling with us this morning? The crackdown is so real.

Cavity search! my brain screams at me, as the bus stops, the doors fly open, and half the passengers get off. The CSO stands there, looking at me with quite a bit of hatred, and that makes me feel very happy—I'm full of Jazz and I am a complete moron. I'm fine with that. I don't care. *You fucking moron!* But my brain's not in the driver's seat and I'm smiling, not giving a crap. I'm waiting for him to grab my arm and scan my ID. It will be a fucking relief when he does. Then he remembers his target; I can see the struggle in his eyes. He turns around, sees that the Shadow has left with the crowd, and jumps off the bus.

The doors shut and the bus takes off. Then I hear someone say, "That was a cruel thing to do." It's the older man in the suit. He's not angry, but sad. I'm about to tell him to mind his own fucking business, when my brain locks back into pilot position and I realize what I've done: I've provoked the CSO, made him furious and violent, just as he's about to arrest the grief-eyed Shadow. I stare out the window to see her walking quickly away from the bus, her fists clenched, still searching for whatever it is she's lost, oblivious to the CSO pushing through the crowd toward her.

Alex and I stand there, stunned. I can't even look at her, I'm so ashamed. She doesn't look at me either, and we walk to the back of the bus to one of the many empty seats and sit on opposite sides. She's angry at me for what I've done; I'm angry at her for being angry at me. It's stupid—that's how it is.

We sit there, stewing, for the next half hour. When the bus pulls into the Zone F Transit Station, I'm still buzzed, and also kind of depressed. I don't want to get off the bus and go through the motions of our plan—get our interzone patches checked, catch a Mega bus to Zone C, go shopping, make fun of rich people buying froyo that would cost me two days of work units. I see that Alex looks depressed too, and that she's still irritated with me, which is good, because I'm still irritated with her. The bus door flings open and we shuffle down the aisle toward the back exit.

As I approach the steps, I hear a quiet voice behind me. "My name is Corporation Security Officer L. I need to scan your ID."

Obviously that CSO isn't talking to me, I think, as I start to shake.

I glance to the left and see a hand holding a large Corporate Security Officer ID badge. Then someone grabs my wrist to do a scan and I swing around—in front of me is another undercover CSO I hadn't even noticed. A Shadow CSO, in fact, dressed in a dark suit like a semiprofessional from Zone C, or even Zone B. It's only the really screwed up, self-hating, extra-sadistic Shadows who become CSOs, and they are fucking chilling. Behind me, Alex has been grabbed by another Shadow CSO in a profesh suit. We totally missed them—I guess because we were high, and fighting—and now one of them has got hold of my arm. The exit's a foot away.

"It will go better for you if you don't draw attention to yourself." Officer L says quietly. "Don't run. CSOs are outside both bus doors."

I look behind me at Alex, whose eyes are deep in panic and I mouth the words, "Stay calm." She nods. Her hat is still firmly placed on her head, hiding her concealer-covered Breeder mark. We'll both be okay. They won't necessarily realize Alex is a Breeder, if she just stays calm and does what they say. They only want to scan her ID and maybe ask a few questions.

Officer L pushes me roughly down the bus stairs. I see the uniformed CSOs waiting at the bottom and I twist around to see Alex being pushed down the stairs behind me. One of the uniformed CSOs drags her away, along with the other undercover Shadow CSO, and soon they're in the middle of the crowd and I can't see them anymore. It happens so fast.

"Where are they taking my friend?" I ask Officer L, trying to stay calm. "Our IDs are valid. Scan our wrists again! It's our day off from the plant. We haven't done anything wrong."

And she just says, "Shut up."

I try to wrench free but she's holding my arm really tight,

and she is so strong. I'm dizzy and weak—idiot. I can't think. One of the uniformed CSOs comes up and L salutes him. He walks beside me, holding my other arm. They push me down the platform until we come to a gray office door with a Corp Bus insignia on the front. Inside there are two chairs, a desk with a compwuter on it, and a bed covered in fresh, white sheets.

When I see the bed, I feel a rush of nausea. I fight them and manage to get my arms free and I run toward the door, which has now closed. I scream. I scream so everyone in the bus station will know. And then they're both on me, and L has her hand across my mouth, wedged against my nose so I can't breathe. I try to bite her but can't and she says, "If I take my hand away, will you scream?"

I nod and she smashes her hand harder against my nose and I feel my lungs starting to hurt and I shake my head, side to side, and she releases her hand and I take big, painful breaths. "Let me out," I say. "Please. I'm going to be sick."

"Vomit all over the floor," she says to me. "I don't care. I know why you're sick. I know what you are."

She's looking at me with real hate. I feel a sting of fear and then I calm down: she must be a crazy Mood. Maybe she doesn't know what she's talking about.

Then the uniformed CSO steps between us and says, "Just relax, okay?" He's talking to Officer L, not to me, and I can tell he's angry at having to work with a Shadow, and cranky about having to sort out a kid in a hot room at the Zone F Transit. And I start to think it might be okay. He says to me, "I'm Senior Corporate Security Officer Q. Why don't you take a seat? This will be over with soon and then you can go."

He seems calm, sane, and on my side. I nod—I don't really have a choice. And it's probably better to cooperate. So I sit down.

"Did you check the Grid for any priors?" he asks.

"No, just a basic ID check," L admits and he rolls his eyes and looks at me, muttering "Stupid Shadow bitch" under his breath. He grins at me, and I grin back. L hears him, and her face blushes red around her white, faded Breeder scar, under the Shadow tattoo stamped on top.

I'm already holding my wrist out. He runs the computer's scanner over it and waits for the results. Then he turns to L in irritation. "Grid says he's fine. Why did you call me with a Code 522?"

Officer L looks at me with even more hatred. Then I see her recover: her blush fades, her mouth sets. "I tracked them all the way from the Wall," she says, her eyes bright. "I'm getting this one's friend checked now. You'll see."

L's mobile phone buzzes and, as she answers, Q runs through the units, education, and work history of my fake ID implant. I can see from where I'm sitting that everything's flashing up "Satisfactory" and that my ID belongs to somebody called "Mathew Ellington." My heart beats frantically—Alex and I should have at least learned basic facts about our IDs.

"Enjoy the sewerage plant?" he asks. He looks at the corner of the screen. "Mathew?"

I shrug. "It's work."

"Tell me about it," he says, and smiles. Actually smiles. I'm wondering how I can work this situation.

L is still talking on her phone.

"Do you play sport?" Q asks me.

"Yeah. Football," I say, which is a total lie. I'm crap at just about every sport that has been invented. But I can tell that old

Q, with his big arms and barrel chest, fancies himself a sporty sort of guy.

"Good on you," he says, and smiles again. We've officially formed a man-bond and it makes him happy because he's been brought in here by a fucking Shadow and he hates that.

I'm about to spin some story about the game of football that me and the guys have down at the sewerage plant, and how sporty and manly and excellent it is, when I notice there's silence. Officer L clicks her mobile shut. She looks really, really happy.

"They've finished the exam and the other suspect is a Breeder," she says. I feel something inside me slide. Oh god. Oh, Alex.

Q looks at me and stiffens. "We'll note this on your file, and you'll be called before the magistrate to give testimony at a Corporation Sessions Hearing," he says. "You'll need to give evidence as to whether you were aware of this fact about your coworker and if you were, there will be serious consequences."

He stands up and goes to the door; opens it. I stand up and follow and I'm about to go through when L says to him, "Hey, sir! Just a minute!"

Q turns to her, really pissed off at her being Bolshie with him. "What? We've got his ID. They'll process him back at the Corporation."

She snorts. "I'm not finished with this one. Look at the eyes."

He hesitates. Then he looks at me. He turns to L. "What?"

"Crystal," she says. "I'm sure of it."

He looks back at me and I feel the man-bond between us vaporize.

"Please," I say, and I can see his eyes harden—begging was the wrong move.

"Show me your eyes," he tells me.

I look up. The myth is that people who take Crystal have a tiny red spot, an imprint of the hormones, in the middle of their pupils. The myth is true. For me, at least.

"Fuck," says Q.

L is almost dancing around the room she's so excited. "You'll need to do a body inspection, right?"

Q nods, and L leaves the room as I'm ordered to strip. My face is burning, I take off my pants and shirt and fold them and put them on the table. Then I take off my underpants and put them underneath the folded clothes. I'm hunched over, hiding my groin.

"Stand up. Move your arms to your sides," he says.

I don't move.

"NOW," he says, and I do.

"Spread your legs."

Q nods—his face is bright red—and picks up his mobile. "Get a medical here right away."

L comes back with two more CSOs along with a medical who is wearing blue paper medical robes over his clothes. The CSOs are both carrying Tasers and the medical has an automatic snapped into his belt. One of the CSOs is holding the kind of black bag a medical might carry around. The other one is holding a kidney-shaped bowl containing a syringe and three vials. I'm still standing there naked, my whole body shaking with fear and rage. When I see the bowl and the bag, I get so terrified I start to piss myself. I can't help it. At least I don't cry.

The medical stares at my groin as piss runs down my legs and forms a hot puddle on the tiles. Then he turns to L and says, "Very good. You can assist me with the Investigation."

L holds me still while the medical gives me an injection and one of the other CSOs opens the black bag and starts to take out a row of instruments, laying them out on the desk beside the computer.

"Lie down on the bed," L tells me.

"Go fuck yourself!" I tell her. I'm crying now.

The medical walks over and smacks me across the face so hard something clicks in my neck and my nose gushes blood. I get on the bed and lie down. The medical uses the first instrument and I don't tell them anything. At least, I think, I've been caught by security while using a fake ID. The fake information will slow them down; it will take them longer to connect me back to Ma, and by tonight, Ma will know something is wrong and will be on the move. But in my heart I know that's not true—Ma would never leave without me. Then the medical gives me another injection and uses the next instrument and I sob with pain but I still don't tell them anything. After the third instrument, I give them my real name and address. I give them Ma's name. I tell them about Alex and her mother. I give them the name of the smuggler at the plant who used to supply my medication and I tell them everything I know about the Book Shadow, and everything I know about Rob, including his full name, which floats into my mind and out of my mouth when the pain gets so bad.

Afterward, I sit there shaking and sobbing, so ashamed I want to die, while L punches the details into the computer, her eyes glistening with happiness. Then she picks up her mobile. "This is Corporate Security Officer L8466, authorized by Superintendent 84."

I fade in and out, woozy from the drugs. All I can hear is L's voice. "I need three Teams, Code 667. First address is 43 Modden Place, Zone F, 7493. Suspect's name is Michael Fuller. Suspected smuggler. Second address is 598 Kootingal Drive, also Zone F, 7493. Suspect's name is Jessica Meadows. Suspected facilitator. Third address is in Zone A and needs to be unlocked, it belongs to Corporation member Robert A. Hunter. Yes, a full Corporation member."

I drag myself off the bed and my legs buckle. The two support CSOs run forward and I push against their bodies. One of them shoves me and I fall back into a chair, red and black crackers going off in my eyes. L's voice drones on. "Yeah, I've got the main suspect with me. Well, send a chopper, then. You're looking for Jessica Meadows. Western appearance. Five foot ten inches."

My stomach heaves and I lean over and vomit. I vomit again. I pass out.

I'm woken up by her voice. "Have you got her? A goat? You're fucking kidding me! May as well get her on animal possession as well. Did you find the Crystal? Awesome."

•

I'm cuffed and taken out the door. Around me the usual Zone F midday crowd throngs around the Transit, busy with errands and shopping and work, oblivious to the torture that has happened in the room behind me. Ten feet away, I see another clump of CSOs and Alex, all tiny, in the middle of them. She is still wearing her hat. Beneath it, her face is bleeding and there's a massive purple egg on her forehead. She sees me and I open my mouth to tell her to say nothing, and to do nothing, when she starts fighting them. She's yelling, "He hasn't done anything! Leave him alone!" They're telling her to shut the fuck up. She breaks away and screams, "Help us! Someone!"

The commuter crowd keeps moving. I see one man look at Alex and slow down; his eyes are kind as he sees her distress, but when he notices the CSOs chasing her, he starts walking quickly away and out of sight. Help is not coming.

Alex runs toward an escalator that leads up to the food court.

All the CSOs take out their Tasers and they're yelling at her to stop but she keeps running. They shoot their Tasers and she dodges past a group of people who are screaming and throwing themselves to the ground, some getting hit by the Tasers. And now she's halfway up the escalator and my heart is flying up there with her and I'm sure she's going to make it. Then the medical steps in front of me and takes his pistol out of his belt and shoots Alex in the back, and Alex tumbles down the escalator and lies crumpled at the bottom.

I take off toward her and they're on me and I kick and punch and fight them as hard as I can, trying to get to her, and I get hit in the face and feel hot blood flushing out and the pain is unreal, and I still fight to get to Alex, and then someone pushes me and I'm on the floor and someone kicks me and someone else comes over and they kick me too and I get kicked again and again and again and again and again.

•

When I come to, I'm bouncing along in the back of a truck. I can't see out of my right eye, my nose feels like it's hanging off my face, and every jolt of the truck makes me want to spew.

My hands are shackled tight in front of me—a chain around my waist connecting me to the wall of the truck. I look up and a CSO I haven't seen before is sitting opposite me, his eyes half shut with sleepiness, and Officer L is on his left. She sees I'm awake, leans over and looks me full in the eyes and says, "Alright?"

My legs are free so I kick at her and miss and my right leg just wobbles in place and she laughs and picks up another syringe and plunges it into my leg, and the truck's going faster and faster as I pass out.

I come to and vomit and there's only black bile now, and a stinging pain in my gut. L curls her lip at the stench and then moves to the partition that separates us from the driver and starts chatting. The sleepy CSO is still slumped sideways, his eyes closed. I look out the window and through the rain see we're on an old stone road and up ahead, lit by flood lights, looms the sixty-foot figure of the Rator. Beyond that, there's a circular sandstone building.

We approach the Rator first. I feel so heartsick that I hope we're heading there, where I can just give in and be burnt up, and never have to feel anything else again.

But the truck keeps going, and we approach the Circle, where all the reeducation programs take place. It's at least thirty stories high and along each level I can see the square dots of tiny, lit windows braced by prison bars.

L bangs on the partition. "No, not General! We want the south side of the Circle, the Incubator," she yells. "She's a Breeder."

"I'm not!" I scream. "Take me to General. Or to the fucking Rator!"

Officer L grins at me, and prepares another syringe. The

truck veers off the main road and we're bumping along a rockier, steeper path. I feel the sting in my arm and then blankness.

•

I come back to consciousness and take a big breath and that hurts—there's a wracking pain in my chest. I'm lying flat on a bed with a sheet over me and I go to push away the sheet, but my wrist and ankles are strapped to the bed. I pull against the straps as hard as I can. I make the bed shake, and the sheet slides off. Under the sheet I'm naked, and there are bandages stuck all over me. My body has a medical smell.

The bed is pushed against a concrete wall in a tiny square room. The room has three concrete walls, with a clear sliding door along the fourth side, facing the interior of the building. Through the sliding door, at the center of the Incubator, I can see the concrete surveillance tower. Behind the tower, opposite me, are more curved rows of transparent doors—in a semicircle around the central tower. I'm in the Circle. The northern semicircle is for reeducation, and the southern is for incubation. Some of the rooms are lit up and some are dark, and as I watch, I see the shadows of people moving around their box cells, identical to mine.

To the left of me there's a toilet with no seat and no lid, and next to that there's a basin with a dull mirror and next to that is a pipe, high on the wall, with a hose attached to it, which I guess is supposed to be the shower. Hanging from the ceiling are rows of metal nozzles that must be fire extinguishers. There's one outward-facing window, about the size of my hand. Everything is gray concrete: the floor, the bed, the walls, the toilet, the window frame—everything except the shower head and sprinklers, which are made of steel. And there's a plastic table and chair in front of the bed, and an intercom speaker, I notice, just above the sliding door. Next to the intercom is a camera, and both the camera and intercom are surrounded by a protective metal cage so I can't knock them out with my shoe or my fists, which is the first thing I want to do.

Then I remember: Alex. Ma. Cranky. The pain comes pushing up inside me and there's the sound of screaming and it's me, and then there are two figures in orange suits standing outside the door and the door opens and they're on me, and then there's a sharp pain in my arm.

•

Crystal has a short half-life, and by the time I wake up again, I'm in withdrawal. I can't tell whether it's night or day, or how much time has passed, but I'm nauseated and have a shocking headache.

I look back through the sliding door at the surveillance tower in the center and the lit-up cells around the periphery. There are hundreds and hundreds of cells, silhouettes moving inside them. I can see nine levels above me, and I don't know how much higher the Circle goes, or how many levels there are below. Could be twenty. Hours pass and the lights of individual cells go on and off, off and on, like a slow signaling system I don't understand.

I'm no longer shackled. I sit up on a thin mattress that's resting on a high, concrete bed and feel a spike of dizziness. My throat hurts. "Hello!" I croak, and my voice bounces off the walls and echoes back to me. I don't know if the speaker above the door records my voice. I don't know if anyone can hear me.

The camera pans to focus on me and there's a click of the

intercom: "You have no speaking privileges. Do that again and you'll be disciplined."

"But there's been a mistake," I say, trying to stay calm. I think about the other times I've tried to fight a Corp decision and how important it is to stay calm, to talk to the most senior person, and to work out what exactly they want, so you can give it to them. "I need to speak to whoever's in charge."

Another click and the voice. "You need to stop speaking now, or you'll be disciplined."

I know I have to stay calm. But I start shaking, and I shout: "There's been a serious mistake! I'm not a Breeder! I need to speak to someone in person." My voice is high and trembling.

A click and the voice. "You need to stop speaking now, or you'll be disciplined."

"Yes, but . . ."

I hear a hiss and look up and see there's a sprinkler head right above the bed and it opens and showers me with water. It's frigid cold. It's all over me and soaking into the sheets. Bastards.

"Could you just . . ."

Water comes down harder. I'm shaking from the cold. I stop talking. I shut my mouth.

The water shuts off.

The intercom clicks. "I'm going to leave you in that cold water for a couple of hours," the voice says. "Then I'll send in some towels and a change of clothes. This is part of your discipline."

•

I hear a click and the voice says, "If you don't take the pills, we're going to have to use the gas. It's up to you."

It's the same metallic voice as before. Is it the same person or different people talking through a computer? I'm standing at the mirror in my room. Behind me, on the table, there are ten pills in bright candy colors laid out on a white plastic plate. Hormones, probably. Medication to quiet me down.

A lot of time has passed. A week or more, maybe. The nausea and headaches are still there and, worse than that, my body is changing. Though I've never had a five-o'clock shadow or even stubble on my face, since I turned eleven and started Crystal, I've had an angular, narrow face. Now when I look in the crappy, wavy mirror stuck to the wall, I can see my face already filling out—looking soft and rounded. Worse than that—much, much worse—is that my chest is filling out too. My nipples itch and the skin around them is starting to swell. It—my body—is so, so disgusting. I want to climb out of it.

The click again, and the voice says, "If you don't take the pills, we're going to have to use the gas."

"I'm not a Breeder!" I shout up to the ceiling, trying to stay calm. "You *have* to understand! Can you please, *please* get whoever is in charge here to come speak to me? My units are in credit. I'm not a Breeder!"

The click again, and the voice says, "If you don't take the pills, we're going to have to use the gas."

I turn back to my bed and to the little table next to it. I walk up and choose the pill closest to the edge, the prettiest—it's purple and blue. I place my index finger behind it and flick it onto the ground. It makes a little tapping sound as it bounces over the concrete. I feel the first flicker of joy that I've felt since I regained consciousness in this hellscape.

Then I go down the row and flick each pill onto the floor. They rattle around like teeth. I feel more joy.

Then another click, and the voice says, "Do you think you're a clever person? That was not a clever thing to do."

I hear another click and a hissing sound, and clouds of gray gas start puffing through the sprinkler heads in the ceiling. *Worth it.* A cloud of gas fills my head. I thrash, knocking the plate off the table, overturning the table, kicking the chair to the wall. I start to wobble and grab the side of the bed to stay upright. The door slides open and two figures in orange suits float in and I try to punch them but my arms are porridge, and then there's a sharp pain in my arm and more fucking black.

•

The first house I remember living in was literally built into the Wall. From the outside, it just looked like a run-down old shack, but once you entered, the crappy, wooden structure made way for extra rooms that had been carved and dug into the twenty-foot-deep stone. It meant we could hide people there, from time to time.

By the time I was five years old, I could put my own mask on and climb onto the roof of the shack and then scramble up to the top of the Wall and look out into the badlands. I could see the huge Corp exploration machines on their missions, in search of viable land and safe water, which it seems they never found. I wanted more than anything to lead one of those crews someday—to go far beyond the horizon into the badlands, into the unknown. I could see myself at the helm, navigating with a compass like Ma had taught me, taking us farther into the difficult terrain—maybe someday even finding another settle-ment. Together, me and my crew would find a new land and build a new world. One where the earth and water were safe. But it would never happen—Westies were forbidden from being on the crews. Up there, I could also see the Corporation Protection machines, digging and building layers of additional stone-and-wire security beyond the Wall, strengthening the boundaries to prevent the Westie masses getting in. I could only see about a quarter mile into the distance, and then the thick brown clouds of dust and pollution blocked my view—the people and the land disappeared.

I used to come inside for dinner, my head full of the huge machines and the thin, brown line of the horizon.

"What's *really* out there?" I asked Ma.

"The whole burned-out world," she said.

"What's it like?"

"Nobody knows now. Nobody can say."

"I'll go there one day. I'll find out."

Ma hit me with her tea towel. "Don't be so silly."

•

I wake up, strapped to my bed, with an IV plugged into the top of my wrist. The entertainment plug has been dug out—I can no longer feel its little plastic rectangle under my skin. My chip is still there. I can feel drugs being pumped into my system, making me swollen and alien. The nausea is unreal. I wriggle as hard as I can and free my right arm. Then I reach over and tug on the IV.

The click, and the voice says, "Let go of the IV, or we will have to use the gas."

I give the IV a good yank and there's a throbbing ache, and then I tug again and the IV flies out of my arm. There's a satisfying spurt of blood, which sprays the wall and soaks into the white sheets.

Another click and the sprinklers hiss and I smell gas. I free my other arm and start to pull on the straps around my legs when my mind starts to numb and cloud. The orange suits stomp in, and there's a sharp pain in my arm. One of the orange suits has a mustache; the other is a Shadow. I clock the weapons around each belt around their waists—baton, Taser, semiautomatic pistol—before all goes black.

•

I wake up and I'm back in bed with the IV stuck in my wrist, and now there are shackles around my wrists and ankles, as well as thick, fabric bands binding my torso to the bed so I can't lift my arms. I push and pull against the restraints as hard as I can, my wrists bleeding, tears of rage burning my eyes.

The click again, and the voice says, "We need to turn your body so you don't get bed sores. We need you to lie there quietly while we do this, or we'll have to use the gas."

I don't answer. The sliding door opens and two orange suits come in. One unlocks the shackles while the other stands there with a syringe ready. The first lifts the sheet around my body and unties the bands. She doesn't look me in the eyes. I wonder how she feels, tying and untying helpless people like me all day. Maybe she has a black box in her head, like I did when I was a Breeder runner—a place to stash away all the awful things she does. I push her away and grab the IV and tug at it, trying to tear it out. She grabs my arms and pushes me back on the bed. She's strong and still doesn't look at me. The other suit comes at me with the syringe, there's a pain in my arm, and my mind goes dark.

.

Every time the gas hisses, I go totally blank. And then I dream. I dream and I remember things.

I've always had trouble sleeping. Even as a tiny kid, I had nightmares: a yellow demon wrapped around a chair, ghosts slithering under the bed. I only half believed in demons and ghouls, but Ma was a true believer. I could see it in her eyes when I told her about the devils that crawled around my room and taunted me in the dark.

She was scared, I could tell. She said to me, "Snap out of it, Will. You have to stay strong."

"I can hear them, Ma," I told her. "I can hear them talking. They wake me up."

Ma believed in demons, but she was always practical—she offered to get me some earplugs.

When the gas hisses, the devils that I haven't seen in years come back.

Tits! they hiss. *We can see your tits, you fucking Breeder!*

You're here for the next twenty years, Will, they say. *They'll make you squeeze out twenty babies.*

I wake up gasping, reaching out, trying to fight something or someone.

The worst thing isn't the nightmares. The worst thing is the vivid memories of Alex, and of Ma—simple things like Alex's bright eyes laughing at me, or Ma's soft hands covering mine. The memories rush at me in the night with such realism, and then I wake up with the ache of missing them.

When I was seven, I had a friend called Brock, who was ten. A kid that much older was like a god to me, and I was thrilled he wanted to hang out. He called me *little freak*, because when we first met he saw me balancing on top of the Wall, staring out at the badlands.

"You're going to break your neck, little freak!" he yelled in delight. We were forbidden to take risks like that. If you fell and broke a leg as a Westie, you were as good as crippled for life—there's no way the Corp was going to spend valuable units fixing up a complex fracture for someone in Zone F.

We used to scramble up and down the Wall and look out at the badlands, planning pirate missions to hold up the Corp vehicles and take all their stuff. Brock's family were smugglers and thieves, like a lot of the people who lived in Zone F, and he had a lot to say about how to hold up a Corp operation. Ma had no problem with people doing what they had to do to survive, but she hated Brock's family, and she told me outright not to play with him. She said that Brock's father was a known snitch, who shopped people for units. She also said that Brock wasn't quite right—there was something "off" about him—and that it was weird he wanted to hang around with me, a kid three years younger than he was. I thought Brock was funny, and besides that, he had his own pocketknife, so I kept playing with him—I just didn't tell Ma.

Feral cats still roamed Zone F back then, and whenever Brock saw one, he'd try to catch it. He told me he'd do "experiments" on any cats he caught, but the only time I saw Brock catch one, it scratched his face off. I wanted to see what Brock would do, how far he would go.

One day, before nightfall, Brock led me to the "Breeder house" at the end of our street. The house had been abandoned long before anyone could remember. The local teenagers said that a Breeder who'd escaped the Incubator once lived there with her six secret kids, until someone tipped off security. One night, she killed them all in their sleep, then she killed herself. The teenagers wouldn't go inside—said the house was haunted.

At first, we just stood in front of the Breeder house, staring at it. The house felt terrible, even from the sidewalk. Both its front windows were smashed and the grass went up past our waists. The house looked like it would be dark and wet inside. There'd be a smell—not of cooking and washing but a wet, hurt smell.

I wanted to go home.

"Come on!" Brock shouted, and he went bounding through the grass, around to the back of the house. I followed him—I didn't have a choice.

The window above the back door was cracked and Brock put his arm through the hole, moving slowly around the slicey bits of glass. The handle clicked and the door flapped open and we stood there. Even Brock just stood at the threshold. I could feel the cold air of the Breeder house on my face; a little shiver went down my back.

Then Brock shoved me, and I lost my balance and fell inside. I stumbled over the linoleum, my hands reaching out, wanting to get my balance, but also not wanting to touch anything. I was surrounded by big dirty shadows. Brock laughed at me.

I kept going, through the empty living room, and, to show him I wasn't scared, through to the kitchen. My eyes adjusted and I could see a table, chairs, a bench. A big, sad gap where the fridge used to be.

"What are you doing over there?" Brock called out.

"Nothing."

Brock came over to me. He took his knife out of his back pocket and flicked it open. *Whiippt.* His eyes were bright.

He carefully folded the knife back into itself. Then he flicked it open again.

He held the knife in front of my face. I thought about the cats and I wished that I were home again. I wished Ma knew where I was. I wished her shift had finished early and she was coming to get me because she somehow knew where I was.

"See the blood on the floor?" Brock said, and shoved me.

There was a big, brown circle. It could be anything—mud, or rust. I nodded anyway—it wasn't worth pissing him off. He reached out and squeezed my arm.

"See that doorway?" he said, pointing down the hall.

"Yeah. Duh."

He smacked my head. "Shut up, freak. She came through there. All the kiddies, sitting around the table, having their dinner. She came up behind them with her knife."

Everyone knew she killed the kids in the middle of the night, when they were sleeping.

He opened the top kitchen drawer next to the sink.

"See the drawer full of knives?" Brock said.

There was nothing there. "Sure," I said.

Brock looked at me. He flicked his pocketknife open and shut a few times. Then he put me in a headlock.

"Strip," he said.

"What?" My heart was pounding.

"You heard me! Everything off!"

Taking my clothes off was unthinkable. I never did it in front of anyone, not even Ma. I never took PE classes, so I never had to get changed at school—Ma gave me a note that said she preferred I use the time to work, and the Corp was more than happy for me to do some extra Manual Processing instead.

Brock pushed the knife nearer to my face. "I mean it. Strip." His eyes were glittering.

He put the knife on my collarbone. He pushed and I felt a sting and we both looked at the blood. Only a bit of blood, but it was right there, on my skin and on the knife.

"Shit," he said. But he wasn't scared. He was thrilled with himself. "Take off your shirt, or I'll cut you again. I'll really do it!"

He would do it, we both knew that. I took off my shirt and threw it on the ground. He came over and kicked it away. It made him even more thrilled.

"I don't know why you and your ma are so stuck-up," Brock said. "My dad says there's something suspect about you just turning up here. Out of nowhere." It wasn't unusual for people to show up in a new part of Zone F, but Brock was right that Ma could be stuck-up, and it set people against her.

"How old's your ma, anyway?" Brock asked, grinning.

I didn't answer. "Take off your jeans," he said.

I took off my jeans and threw them down. I stood there in my underpants.

"Wanna know what my dad says *you* are?" Brock said.

I felt something inside me crack.

"Take off your underpants, little freak!" Brock shouted. "My dad says you're a . . ."

And that's when I kicked him. I swung my leg up and kicked him so hard, right in the nuts. He was on the ground, so I kicked him again. I wasn't a freak. I was going to be a successful Westie someday—much more successful than Brock. A proper job, a house, a Shadow. I'd show them all.

Then Brock reached up with his knife and slashed my arm from elbow to thumb.

They say that I screamed so loudly, lights went on up and down the street. Suddenly, Brock's father was in the room. Brock's father carried me home and wrapped my arm in a clean rag, and then they all waited with me for Ma to come home from the plant.

The next thing I remember is waking up in my own room. On the bedside table was a bubble strip of painkillers and a glass of lemonade. It was the middle of the night, and there was no traffic. The only sound was the buzz of a streetlight. I started to cry but couldn't think why—I just felt unbearable sadness.

I didn't go to school the following day, and we moved away from that house the next night.

When we got to the new place, it was another dirty and broken rental in another part of Zone F. We moved four more times after that. Each time, we had to get the security chips cut out of our wrists and new ones sewn in. We got new IDs, new unit profiles and new names. Each time, our unit level plummeted as we traded the surpluses Ma had painstakingly saved for new lives. First, I was Will Grover, then I was Stephen Elliott, then I was Keats Tyrell, and then Adam van Glusser. The last time we moved, Ma let me choose my name for the first time: *Will*, I told her. *I want to be Will again, the name my mother gave me*. I became Will Meadows.

•

I hit puberty at age eleven. Until that point, everyone thought of me as a boy, and this was how I thought of myself too. A boy who was working toward a future. Ma must have decided to pass me off as a boy when she bought my first fake ID, as a newborn, but she never told me why she did it. I'm guessing she didn't want to lose me to the Corp, like she lost my mother when she was only seven. Or maybe she decided that, while life in the Corp is hard for all Westies, it's more bearable to live here as a male. All I know is, Ma never, ever called me a boy or a Breeder. When she brought it up, she would say to me, "We have to be careful about *your condition*." I think she was scared that if we actually talked about it, I'd accidentally say the word "Breeder" to someone. As it turned out, I never felt strongly that I was either a boy or a Breeder, so living as a boy was just fine with me. I don't think I could have survived going to a Preincubator Center as a little kid. But then, who does, really, survive it?

When I hit puberty, Ma completely lost her mind, and for a while, Ma actually locked me up. *Locked* me inside our tiny house while she was at work, and wouldn't let me out of her sight when she was home. It was traumatic—suddenly, I couldn't do whatever I wanted. Suddenly, I couldn't roam the streets with all my friends. I hated my Breeder body: really, really hated it. I blamed it for all the crappy things I had to put up with: the terror that I was going to be discovered by a CSO and burned in the Rator; or stolen by a Waster and raped and murdered; or worse, taken to the Incubator and made into a baby machine for the Corp. I blamed it for the way men and boys looked at me. There was a growing softness around my hips and stomach, and I had *breasts*. My body bled out of nowhere. I felt like it was attacking me. And then Ma found out about Crystal 8, and all the bad Breeder stuff went away. My body went back to normal. I was allowed out of the house again. I could run the streets freely. Nobody was going to kidnap me or rent me out to the Corp. I could live as myself again. I could live as a person.

We moved again—that's when I became "Adam van Glusser"—and I was secretly a Crystal 8 boy. I learned how to pick out other Crystal boys like me. The Crystal made us thin and some of us even grew slight mustaches, but I could always tell. There weren't many of us. There were never any in my class or in my neighborhood—sometimes I'd pass one on the Transit. I'd want desperately to talk to them, to send a sign, but it was too dangerous. I'd just watch them, and think *Goodspeed*, hoping the best for them with all my heart, and then I'd walk on.

I was still Adam when I met Sommer. She was the only Breeder left in our grade—we were both twelve years old.

I wanted to be Sommer's best friend from the first time I saw her.

Sommer's parents were rich—rich for Zone F, anyway. She was a quick, smart-mouthed, skinny kid with fast hands, and she was tougher than most of the boys. Sommer lived with her Shadow mother and her father in a two-level house. Her parents must have done a lot of illegal stuff to be able to keep her at school and out of the Incubator, because in addition to Breeders being Dead Units—they're not allowed to generate any credit outside the Incubators—their families are charged an annual Breeder Tax of one thousand units once they turn six years old. Even Breeders who weren't sent to Preincubation programs were kept home from school by the time they were eight, so as not to ratchet up education debt for their families. Sommer told me she was never going to the Incubator. Her parents were keeping her home until she was fifteen, she told me, and then she'd go to a Zone C high school to become a profesh. I knew that was impossible—everyone knew that the Corp collected all the Breeders when they turned thirteen years old, no matter how many units their families saved up. But I didn't say that to Sommer.

I asked Ma if we could tell Sommer and her family about Crystal 8, hook her up with the Gray Corps smuggler at the plant who sold Ma my Crystal—help Sommer really stay with her family and go to high school.

"Definitely not, Will," Ma said. She made me promise to keep my mouth shut.

Sommer wasn't embarrassed about being a Breeder. As she hit puberty, she put on big earrings and floofy skirts—she seemed determined to make it even clearer to everyone that she was a Breeder.

The last time I spoke to Sommer, she waited for me outside the school gates and we walked home together because best friends walk each other home, and we were best friends. It was almost dark when we reached the front of my house.

I put my hand on our gate. "See ya," I said to her.

"See ya. Wouldn't wanna be ya," Sommer said, and she winked.

The next day, there was a raid on our Crystal smuggler and Ma was afraid we would be traced. We moved in the middle of the night for the final time. I don't know if Sommer believed right up to the moment she was taken away by the Corp that she was going to Zone C for high school or whether she knew all along that she was going to the Incubator. I like to think that her story was her way of saying *Fuck you* to everyone.

•

"Hey!" I yell, just to hear the sound of my voice. The silence is killing me, and as the sedatives wear off, I'm so fucking bored. I never hear footsteps or the scraping of shoes or muffled voices outside, only the voice from the intercom. I would settle for the sound of shouting, for the sound of nails down a board, for the sound of a fly buzzing. There's nothing. I hum to myself but if I forget and sing too loud, I get the sprinkler.

"Hey!" I yell again, knowing I'll get sprayed. I just want to hear the voice again, I just want to hear another human person— it's worth the hose—but they seem to know that, because no sound comes through the intercom. Instead, another blast from the sprinkler. Bastards.

But then the voice starts. "Think about it. We have a choice with respect to our circumstances. What choices have you made? What exact choices got you here?"

"Hey!" I yell.

The voice starts again. It's a recording that they put on a

loop. I've heard it so many times that it no longer cracks the boredom. "Think about it. We have a choice with respect to our circumstances . . ."

•

I hear the click and the voice says, "Eat the food or we'll force-feed you. It's up to you."

I'm sitting in the chair and on the table is a white plastic tray of food. On the tray there are three squares of different-colored mush: brown, yellow, and orange. Foul. The voice has been telling me that I need to sit up more, to retain muscle tone. I'm on a break from the IV. Instead I have a drug patch in my back that they stitched under my skin while I was in a drug-sleep—no amount of clawing can remove it.

The intercom clicks and the voice says, "Eat the food or we'll force-feed you with tubes. It's up to you."

Fuck that. I sweep the tray onto the floor where it spatters all over the concrete and up the wall. So revolting. So satisfying.

The intercom clicks and the gas comes, and then the orange mustache suit and the orange Shadow suit are in front of the door and the mustache is carrying a long hose with a funnel-thing at the end, and the Shadow is carrying a bottle of something brown. Then they're inside the room and I'm up out of the chair but the man has me around the arms and is holding my jaw and the hose is being forced down my throat with a clawing, wrenching pain.

"Wrong choice," says the orange Shadow.

"You need nutrition," says the orange man.

It feels like scraping and drowning, all at once. It hurts so, so much.

•

I'm five or six years old. It's the middle of the night and Ma's heels click on the floor and she bends over to kiss me goodbye before she leaves for her shift.

"Ma," I say. I'm half asleep.

"Yes, love?"

"Were you really once a Zone C?"

"Yes, love."

"And were you really a profesh?"

"Yes, love."

"And what happened?"

She sighs. "Ah, Will. I have to go to work."

"Please! Ma, you never tell me anything."

She sighs again. "I grew up in Zone C. My parents had saved a lot of units and I had a good childhood. I had to go to the Incubator when I was fourteen. That was the maximum age back then, and my parents could afford to keep me until it was no longer possible. I stayed in the Incubator a long, long time. Then your grandfather came to choose a wife, and he chose me—I was thirty-five. So I left with him. And we had your mother— we were so lucky to have a child. We lived in Zone C, and were happy, until your grandfather died when she was six years old. Cancer. Then, your mother was all I had left—I wanted to keep her with me forever. But we'd spent all our units on his treatment, and didn't have the units to keep her. The Corp came and took her . . ." Ma starts to cry. "Will, I have to go."

Ma was here, once—Ma was in the Incubator, birthing children for the Corporation. She had twenty-one Corporation children for them in twenty-one years. And then my mother was here. She had only one child—me. My mother in a cell just like this. My mother being pumped full of drugs. My mother being forced into pregnancy, forced to have the baby who became me.

•

My chest hurts. There's a lot of soft flesh around the nipples where there used to be flat skin.

I can't stop crying. I press my index finger into my stom ach. Soft. Nauseating.

My body feels sick with not moving. I can't tell whether it's day or night, but I think it's been many weeks that I've been lying here like this. Whenever I open my eyes, I see the concrete watchtower and the floodlights that shine from it, which are always bright, all the time—all the time.

The click and the voice says, "We are willing to try this again. You're the one in charge here. It's your choice."

"Okay," I say, my eyes full of water. I get up out of the bed, shaky because I'm not used to moving. I put on the green track-suit that's folded on the chair next to the bed. I sit down on the plastic chair, in front of the plastic table. I eat the orange mush and leave the brown and the yellow squares untouched. The orange mush is sweet. The texture is viscous and has bits in it—it's like eating crunchy snot.

The intercom clicks. "Now the pills."

It's the same voice. It's always the same voice. I pick up the first pill and put it in my mouth and take a sip of water and swallow. I pick up the next pill and put it in my mouth and swallow.

I need to behave myself. I show all the ways I'm a good Breeder.

•

I wake up and there's breakfast on a tray next to me. Not cubes of mush but real food.

There's a click. "If you keep making the right choices, you'll receive exercise privileges."

"Can I go speak to someone in person, please?"

Silence.

There's a lump of pain in my throat. "Why can't I speak to someone? How many times do I have to tell you? I'm not a Breeder!"

I get the sprinkler.

Click of the intercom. "We will teach you to make better choices."

Fuck better choices.

Click. "You're an important resource for the Corporation.

Fuck that.

"I'M NOT A BREEDER!"

•

I'm being punished with mush again. The tray of food is twice the size of the last one. I eat the orange mush. Then I eat the yellow mush as well. The yellow mush is harder than the orange, and silky because it's full of fat. It's an abomination. The brown mush is the softest—I scoop it up with a spoon and let it dribble back onto the tray.

I'm sleepy, so I get on the bed and curl up under the sheets. When I woke up this morning, they'd changed the sheets during the night while I slept.

"My name's Will," I whisper to myself, very low, so as not to set off the sprinkler. I whisper it again and again.

"My name is Will. I'm a Westie. I live in Zone F. My Corporation account is in credit."

"My name is Will. I'm a Westie. I live in Zone F. My Corporation account is in credit."

"My name is Will. I'm a Westie. I live in Zone F. My Corporation account is in credit."

•

I wake up feeling hot and sticky and throw the sheets aside. There's blood between my legs and in a circle underneath me and all over the sheets and I scream.

There's a click and the gas comes and then the orange suits come. I am bleeding between my legs. I am going to die.

•

I wake up and there's a box on the table. I feel happy, thinking stupidly of the presents that Ma used to get me when I was little—because I'm groggy from the drugs. I look at the box: *Tampons*, it says. Inside, lined up like soldiers, are cotton cylinders covered in plastic. There's a folded informational brochure and I open it. The brochure explains the menstrual cycle and has six drawings describing how to insert a tampon into the vagina.

I tear the plastic off a cylinder, and see that there's a length of string at the end. I use the string to hang the first tampon from the sprinkler. The camera starts to move and I know I'm going to be punished but I don't care. I look up into the eye of the security camera in defiance as it clicks into focus on me as I hang the second tampon. Then the sprinklers start. The water soaks me and the tampons as I tie up two more, and they bloat and swing with the force of the spray. I lie on the bed and watch them. I feel the blood dripping between my legs, seeping into my underpants, as I wait for the orange suits to come through the sliding door.

"I'm not a fucking Breeder!" I scream.

Here they come! I hear their stamping feet. Then, the usual routine: I fight them, they inject me, then all goes dark.

•

I hear the click and the voice says, "We're going to have to start again."

There's a dry feeling between my legs. I put my hand there and there's string sticking out of me. My ankle is tied to the bed and there's an IV in my wrist.

•

There's the click and the voice says, "Eat your food."

I do it. I can't be bothered not doing it.

There's the click and the voice says, "Take your pills."

I do it.

The voice says, "Stand up," and I pull myself up and teeter there, and I wait until the voice says, "You can rest," before I sink back into the chair, exhausted.

The voice says, "Walk up and down the cell, back and forth, until I say stop. This is for your muscle tone."

I get up and walk. I do what they tell me to do.

This goes on for days.

Soon, they return full privileges to me—no more leg ties, no random insertion of IVs. I'm allowed full movement around the cell. My body hurts all over, but that's a welcome distraction compared to what I'm feeling inside.

•

I stand in front of the mirror, looking at the brand down the left side of my face: an embryo, curled into itself like a leaf. They etched it there during one of my chemical sleeps. There are bruises all over my face, purple and yellow, and my nose is off center and my right eye squints.

I have a pale, pudgy face, surrounded by brown curls that come down to the shoulders, and I have a bloated body dressed in a green tracksuit. There are . . . there are breasts. They stick out. There are hips. There's so much fat on this body. Everything is padded and lumpy.

It's my body. But it's not my fucking body.

•

My days are so tedious, I could kill myself. I've been here a long, long, *long* time. Months.

I'm so obedient that they've stopped tying me to the bed, even at night. I eat the mush they give me. I swallow the pills. The orange suits don't come with their injections anymore.

I watch the sliding door.

An orange suit crosses, holding a leash. He holds out a baton with his other hand, the Taser and semiautomatic fixed to his belt.

A Breeder follows him, the leash tied to her wrist, her large belly leading, taut like a balloon shoved up her tracksuit top. I can't see her face. She's followed by another orange suit.

Then I hear noises and realize that they're putting her in the cell next to me. But the weird thing is that I can hear their voices, and I can hear her voice, as they settle her in. Usually, I don't hear anything outside my cell—usually, my cell is sound-proof. There must be some kind of connection between my cell and the cell next door.

·

I can hear the Breeder in the next cell, weeping. Then the voice over her intercom chides her and there's silence.

Now that I can move around the cell freely, I take every chance I get to be close to the wall that connects our two cells. I want to understand why I can hear the Breeder.

I go up to the wall and press my hands against it—for the thousandth time—and I move my legs slowly back and forth, one at a time, pretending to be doing some healthy stretches, and for the thousandth time I see nothing: just a sealed concrete wall.

I curl up onto the bed, lying on my side, and then I see it. Behind the bottom of the bed, someone has dug into the concrete wall to make a tiny tunnel the diameter of a half dollar, reaching into the next cell. It must have taken them months. Did they dig either side until they met in the middle? Were they friends? Is it possible to have a friend in here?

A couple of hours later, the Breeder next door starts sobbing again, then she's screaming. I run up to the sliding door but can't see anything. I go back and curl up on the bed, my back to the camera, so the camera can't see me talking.

"Hey!" I whisper, and the howling stops. "Are you alright?"

"Of course I'm not fucking alright!" comes the voice—a spitting, harsh voice, as though her throat has been torn.

"Shhh," I say. "They'll just come and drug you."

She wails. The sound is awful. I hear the door of her cell opening and the stomping of the orange suits.

•

I wake up to a sniffing sound. I drape myself over the bed and lower my head. Fuck it. "Hello?" I whisper.

"Hello," she says. Her voice is still ragged.

"Are you okay?" I ask.

"No," she says. "No."

"My name is Will," I say. It feels so good to say my name. I want to keep talking. "What's your name?"

"Mary," she says. She starts to weep.

"Shhh," I say, my heart smashing in my chest. "They'll come for you."

"The baby died," she says. "It's the fifth one I've had, and they've all died. I'm going to the Rator for sure."

Fuck.

"How many months are you?" she asks me.

"I'm not a Breeder," I tell her. "They made a mistake."

"Yeah, right. How long have you been in here? Nine months? Ten?"

"Right. But I'm not a Breeder."

"They inseminate you when you're sedated," she says. "You don't even know it's happened."

"Yeah but I'm not . . ."

"You *are*, or you wouldn't still be in this unit."

"I'M NOT!" I yell. I jump off the bed, away from her. Behind me, I can hear Mary laughing.

I look down at my protruding stomach and feel the heat of shame rush to my face. All the ways I've been pretending won't work anymore.

I kick over the chair, tear the sheets and blankets off my bed, and throw my toothbrush across the room. Everything else in the cell is either concrete or bolted down and I need to destroy. So I go about destroying myself: I smash my whole body against the concrete wall, and then run to the other side of the cell and drive myself into the wall again and again and again.

I curl up on the floor, around my giant belly, my hands to my ears.

I want to die. I want to die.

There's no comfort coming. I keep thinking it's coming but it isn't.

All the young Breeders outside the wall thought comfort was coming too. And instead they saw me—me dragging them beyond the Gray Zone, loading them into Rob's car, sending them to the Incubator.

I recite their names to myself.

The girls I smuggled in, to this fate.

To remember.

Kylie, age fifteen, with her angry fists.

Darcy, age thirteen.

Clarice, age fifteen, and Mai, age fourteen.

Kim, age twelve, and Sophie, age thirteen.

Daniella, age twelve, clutching her pink rabbit.

There are hundreds more.

There are so many.

They're all in here with me—in the Incubator somewhere. I did that to them in order to keep myself safe.

There is no safe place.

I grab the bottom sheet from my bed, get up on the plastic chair, tie the bed sheet around the sprinkler head, hoist my neck through the loop. I hesitate, then see my pregnant stomach again, and then I kick back that fucking chair as hard as I can.

Shudder up my spine, above my heart, down my legs. Lungs compress, my limbs jerk. Fear. Then nothing.

•

There's movement beneath me. A sharp light in my eyes.

"No. Put her over there."

A rolling motion, a shooting pain in my neck.

"Dammit, be gentle with her spine!"

Another bright light in my eyes.

Then there's a face in front of mine. Bright green eyes above a surgical mask. "We've had to operate. You stupid little Breeder. But you should be able to walk."

A cold stinging in my arm, then darkness.

I drift in and out of consciousness. I'm so, so tired. When

I'm awake, I sense pieces of sound and light, like in dreams. And then I'm out again.

I wake to real music. Not an entertainment plug. It hurts my heart, it's so beautiful.

And there's a light, a different kind of light. It's warm. Right above me are angels: the tumbling, laughing, happy, beautiful angels, just like the Book Shadow had in her shop, but ten times larger, and so bright. Are they real? Ma used to tell me about what she called "Heaven"—a place, she said, where she believed we go when we die. A place filled with angels, one for each of us. It's where everything lost is returned; where everyone sought is found; where the answer to every sorrow is love. I've never believed in Heaven, to be honest. Even if there *is* life after death, I bet it would be like here anyway—a place that calculates your units earned and your units owed, and if you're in deficit, makes you *pay*.

It all goes dark again.

When I wake, the voice is warm.

"You're awake, are you?" I'm wrapped in something soft.

I try to focus my eyes on something. I see a wall. There *are* angels: the angels aren't real but painted on the wall. The music stops. I'm in a bed wrapped in a thick, heavy blanket.

I look at the huge, tight belly that is part of my own body. I failed—I'm still here. I'm still attached to that Thing. I try to sit up but am shackled again.

"Don't move." The voice is to the right and I try to turn my head but can't. "No, don't turn your head. Let your muscles go slack."

The voice sounds musical, rich, older. "You're doing really well. You're safe."

Yeah, right. A face comes into view: those bright green eyes again. I try to talk, but there's too much pain.

"Take it easy." The mask comes off. "Just relax. Really."

She's female, but she has no scar or tattoo. She looks male and female, old and young, all at the same time—she has a beautiful face, like from one of the Book Shadow's old-timey painting books, but her expression is as calm and untraumatized as a man's.

"Where am I?"

"In my home. In Zone A." It's one of the biggest rooms I've ever seen. There are paintings on the walls and the doors at the end open up into bright sunlight.

"Are you a magistrate?" I ask. My voice is hoarse and it hurts to talk.

She laughs at me.

"Are you a . . . Shadow?"

There's another laugh. "Only Westies are Shadows. I'm Professor Keeling, the surgeon of the Incubator. I've had to make a small adjustment to your spine as a result of your—suicide attempt. And I'm also your obstetrician."

My face goes hot. "You operated on me? Here?"

She nods and points to a hallway behind us. "I have a full surgery room out there, and private recuperation rooms."

She's looking at me carefully. Do all Breeders get lifted into Zone A when they try to destroy themselves? She *wants* something. She's waiting.

"Will, I can't emphasize enough what a valuable resource you're carrying. As you know. And we're very interested in a live birth."

I don't say anything. Ma always taught me not to give

anything away for free: to find the angle with a person, to find out what they want, and then to use that as leverage. But the Corp already has everything they want from me—there's nothing I can hold back.

"What do you want?" I ask.

"I *love* Westie directness," she says, and smiles. "I've brought you here to monitor you myself. Is there anything I can bring you to make you more comfortable?"

"I need some information about my family," I tell the surgeon.

She shakes her head. "I can't give you anything like that," she says, still smiling.

I'm angry at how disappointed I feel, it's like another kick in the guts. "Then why bother asking?"

She stops smiling and looks completely deadpan. Her expression chills me.

"It would be good for you if we could get along, Will, until we get that live birth. It won't be long now, but I'm going to keep you here until that happens. So just be a good Breeder, okay?" I hear the crackle of plastic and then there's a sharp, cold pain in my arm. "I'm just going to give you this to calm you down. It's very important that we protect your spine."

I start to fade out as the music resumes. It's definitely not on an entertainment plug. Somebody is playing a real instrument.

But the last thing I hear is the surgeon's voice. "I have a significant interest in you, Will. We'll be seeing a lot of each other."

•

The night I was born, Ma came home from work and found my mother dead. Ma heard some weak crying and found me, wrapped in an old T-shirt and tucked into the top drawer of my mother's bedside table. On top of me was the note: "Baby Name Will." I had that note for years, covered in plastic and tucked into my underwear drawer, and I took it wherever we moved.

Ma knew it was all over when she saw my mother's body and me and that note. When my mother was sent to a Preincubation Center at seven years old, Ma had told her to be strong, to live out her time and wait for the day when she would be free. But my mother had somehow done the unthinkable: at thirteen, she had broken out of the Incubator and come home, pregnant, to be with Ma. Everything was lost. Ma knew that when the Corp caught up with them—which they would—they'd send both of them to the Rator. Ma never said much about that time, but she did mention that she would never understand why my mother had run away—not when there was no hope that running away would lead to anything but death.

Ma had planned to keep both my mother and me secret—in hiding—until she could get some fake IDs and smuggle us from Zone C into an outer zone. Ma thought she'd hide her daughter and keep her safe forever; that hopefully the baby would be a boy, and Ma would smuggle him into a work unit. But then I was born, and I was a Breeder, and my mother wrecked Ma's plan by killing herself.

Ma held me. She packed a large backpack with clothes, tins of food, and a thick envelope full of cash. She went out to the shed and got a can of old petrol—it was so old she had to prize the lid open with a knife. She took the petrol and went upstairs to the front bedroom, where my mother's body lay on the bed. She wanted to burn it all down, to remove any signs that my mother had been in the house, that a baby had been born—to remove all records relating to my mother, and to Ma herself. Ma took a pocketknife and stabbed her own wrist, digging out the chip. In that chip lay all the units that Ma had painstakingly built up herself. She threw it on the bed. Then she looked for the last time at her daughter, who was still very beautiful and very young.

Ma settled me in the crook of her arm. Then she took the can and, starting in the front bedroom, she poured petrol over her daughter and the bed and the documents, and then the carpet and furniture. As she came out of the bedroom, she heard sirens in the distance. Somebody had already tipped off the CSOs. It would be a crime for neighbors to try to hide trouble, and whoever snitched would have earned a lot of units for it.

Ma took a lighter out of her pocket and then bent down and lit the edge of the pool of petrol. She watched the *whoosh* of flames shoot up the hallway. Then, with sirens screeching in front of the house and me wailing in her arms, she jumped out the second-floor rear window into the yard below; she curled around me so that I was fine, but she broke her leg badly when she landed. With only a backpack of belongings, she spent weeks smuggling me to the edge of the Corp, to Zone F, where she slowly set up a new life. She never contacted her family or friends again. They must have assumed she'd been sent to the Rator.

•

I wake up screaming. Fire pain shooting through the center of my body, tearing me apart.

Searing light.

I feel the shackles loosen and then a figure leans over me and I see the bright eyes of the surgeon.

"No. Leave her shackled. I'll do a C-section," she says.

The pain is unspeakable. Then a cold sting in my wrist and everything goes blank.

●

She. A voice at the end of my bed says, "*She* is seven pounds, two ounces. *She* is healthy."

I don't want to think about it but it's hard when they call her . . . *she*.

They ask if I want to see her. They hold up a bundle at me—a soft rainbow blanket I can't fully see inside. A tiny bundle with some dark hair sticking out at the top. I say no. I tell them to take her away from me. I'm given more drugs, and I feel myself fading again. I'm aware enough to feel myself being lifted and carried to an Incubator van. I want to see outside the house—it would be my first time seeing Zone A—but I'm already woozy. I only see clear skies and some tall stone buildings, thick with beautiful trees, before there's total darkness.

●

I'm back in my cell.

My face is still sore and bruised from where I ran into the wall. My spine aches. I don't fucking care. I don't have a body. They've taken off the hand shackles but the leg shackles remain.

I hear rustling next door.

"Hey," I whisper, toward the gap in the wall.

"Hey back," says a voice. Except it isn't Mary. This Breeder's voice isn't full of tears: it's strong and angry and it's a low, full-bodied voice, completely different from Mary's high, weak one.

"You're new here?" I say.

"Nope."

"Where's Mary?"

"The Rator."

•

In the middle of the night I'm shaken awake by two orange suits who take off the leg shackles and then drag me out of my cell. I'm taken down the hall, then a door bangs open that leads to some cold concrete stairs. I glance at the pistols and batons in their belts and wonder if this is how I'm going to die—getting raped and then murdered by orange suits in a stinking fire escape—and to be honest, I'm not that bothered by the idea. I stumble as they pull me roughly down, down the flights. But when we hit the bottom floor, one of them pushes open another heavy door, and I'm out into the starry night for the first time in almost a year.

A woman is standing there, tall and strong, with short, white hair and high cheekbones. She looks like she must be in her early thirties. She holds out her hand, and I shake it. She takes off her mask. I look around the exit for the security camera, and she watches me—I find it, winking from the eastern corner.

"Don't worry about that," she says. "I have an arrangement." One of the orange suits hands me a mask, and then he and the other suit move around the corner, where they can still see us.

"I'm Cate Cormack," she says. It's the low, deep voice from the cell next to me. "We don't have long. I wanted to speak to you in person."

I nod.

"Will, I'm not going to cushion this. I know you've met with the surgeon. I know she's planning to take you out of the Incubator. I don't know why, but this obviously means that you're a security threat to us."

"But . . ."

She holds up her hand. "Don't explain. Will, you're a threat but also an opportunity for us. It's time for you to choose a side."

I'm afraid of Cate, but also interested. How is it that she knows so much?

"I'm the leader of the Response," Cate says, as if she's reading my mind. "May we all have Goodspeed." Cate makes the sign across her forehead, lips, and heart. It's the same sign that Ma used to make, when she was worried or when there was danger.

"You need to know that some of the orange suits are Responders too," she says. "Westie boys and men are also disposable to the Corp. Just in a different way from girls. And so they're my eyes and ears."

I think of all the guys I've seen sent to the Rator for not making their ever-increasing quotas, and I nod.

From where they stand, the orange men both make a sign across their foreheads, then across their lips and their hearts.

Cate lights a cigarette and hands one to me, and we lean against the cold wall and smoke. I'm looking up at the stars and smoking, and it's a small point of happiness.

Then Cate breaks this moment. "I know you've just had your first live birth, Will."

I look away.

"You shouldn't be ashamed," she says. "These people did

the same to me—pumped me full of hormones, impregnated me against my will."

I nod, but my face burns. Cate reaches over and touches my shoulder. It's the first time anyone has touched me gently in almost a year and I can't help it—I start to cry.

"Will, I've had nineteen births, eleven living. I was smuggled in here by Breeder runners when I was *nine*. They started me on puberty drugs immediately—illegally young, of course, breaking even their own laws."

She sighs. "Can you imagine that, Will? I was just a skinny little nine-year-old. Can you imagine the souls of the people who do this to kids?"

I look away. If Cate finds out I was a Breeder runner, there'll be no end to my hell.

"It's time to stop being sad, and to be *angry*."

"I *am* angry."

Cate looks at me closely. "Will. I know everything that happens in this place. I know you were taken to Zone A to be with the surgeon but I don't know why. I know you tried to kill yourself . . . I've never known her to take a suicide to Zone A before."

"I don't know why either. She just said she wanted a live birth."

Cate seems like somebody who is good at reading people—I can see her trying to decide about me.

"I also looked into your history, Will. I can't find anything before two aliases somebody made for you—Adam van Glusser and Keats Tyrell. Why did you have aliases? Were you involved in the Response?"

She looks so serious; I feel like laughing.

I shake my head.

"Then what?"

I hesitate. I've never told anyone my story. Not even Alex. It's been hammered into me since before I could talk—*Don't tell anyone about yourself. It's too dangerous.* But then something occurs to me. "If you have access to information, is it possible for you to find out about people?"

"That depends. Which people?"

I tell her the full names of Ma and Alex. It feels so good to say them out loud.

"And who are they to you?"

"My grandmother. And my girlfriend."

She grinds her cigarette into the ground with her boot. "First, tell me all about yourself."

I take a breath. Of all the strange things that are happening, telling my story feels like the most bizarre. I'm not used to talking about myself. "Ma hid me because my mother—a Breeder—ran away from the Incubator and killed herself. That's why we had aliases. First, I was Will Grover, and then I was Stephen Elliott."

Cate's face is keen with interest. "What was your mother's name?"

"Her real name? I don't know."

She looks at me with hostility. "I honestly don't," I tell her. "Ma never told me her own real name either. For safety reasons."

"So your grandmother hid you from the Corp and arranged the aliases?"

"Yeah. Then, when I was older, I lived as a Crystal boy. We had to move a lot, when people got close to finding out, which led to more aliases. My grandmother and me—we were each other's entire family."

Cate nods. There are stories about people like me, the Crystal boys, out there among the Westies—even outside the Corporation, beyond the Wall, they know it's an option. She looks at me steadily, still evaluating me.

"Are you sure you didn't grow up in the Response?"

"No, I know nothing about the Response," I say.

I can see Cate decide to trust me, a little. "I know Alex Winterson," she says. "She's here in the Incubator, on one of the upper floors, after having a stillbirth."

It feels so *sudden*—to hear Alex's name spoken by someone else for the first time in over a year; to know she exists outside my mind.

"Is she okay?" I ask.

She shrugs. "Yes."

I can hardly breathe. "Can I see her?"

"If you do something for me, I could arrange for you to see Alex."

"I'll do anything," I say, without hesitation.

"I want you to join the Response. I want your loyalty."

"No problem."

"And another thing: They tell me you have quick hands."

"Yes."

"I need you to get something from the surgeon's place for me."

"How do you know I'll be going there again?"

She raises her eyebrows at me—she's no fool. Which means I need to be extra careful around her. "I think it's fair to assume," she says.

"What do you need?"

"Just a package," she says tersely, meaning *back off*.

I nod—I make it enthusiastic. The truth is, I really will do anything to see Alex. "I'll do it," I tell her. "If it's small enough for me to smuggle out on my body, some tape would be helpful, maybe some elastic band or fabric?"

"I'll get those things for you," Cate says. "In the meantime, let me find the information about your grandmother," she says.

•

Sometimes, we ran Breeders who were under twelve years old across the Wall, and we took them straight to the Incubator. The Gray Corps affiliates got paid and their security chips were forged and that was that. The Breeders who were too small to pass as twelve, we took to one of the Corp's Preincubation Centers. It is also where orphans and foster kids are taken, as well as juvenile delinquents or anyone found on the wrong side of a zone. Some Breeders in these centers are as young as six years old. Rob normally did those drop-offs by himself, but I went with him once. We only had one Breeder to deliver, a small, bright kid named Lucky, who was eight years old. She shook my hand before I loaded her in the back of the SUV, and again when I brought her outside into the warm night air. Since there was only her, Rob stayed in the car while I went up to the door of the large brick veneer house in Zone B. I knocked on the door and a young Breeder answered.

She smiled at me. "Are you bringing us a new friend?" she asked. An adult appeared behind her, a stern-looking Shadow of fifty or so. I hesitated and looked at the Shadow for a sign of how to respond.

The Shadow nodded at me.

"Yes," I said to the young Breeder. "I am." Lucky solemnly shook my hand a final time and was taken away. The Shadow gave me a wad of cash and closed the door in my face without further comment.

When Rob dropped me back to the Gray Zone that morning, I didn't feel like going to the diner, so I walked to the end of the street and climbed over the splintered, white fence to the reservoir. The moon was holding just over the dam, at the bottom of a white sky. The wind was up. I kept walking, straight into the Waster hunting ground—I didn't care. The reservoir was thick with overgrown wattle trees and weeds. It was a rocky, dark place, its trails marked faint and uneven. There was only one proper path, a wide fire track—the others were merely slight indentations, worn down mostly by the Wasters. At the end of the track there was a fork. I took the path to the right, which led down to the water—there were dead cigarettes and condoms strewn about, and food wrappers.

It was a clear, bright night. I could see stars. I took my mask off and could breathe. I lay down across a large rock and looked up at the sky. So many stars! Some of them were satellites, the Book Shadow had told me—human-made machines that had been launched into space in the time Before, broken now but circling the planet forever. I heard the crunching of footsteps across the rubbish and the undergrowth. Then a face above me: Alex.

"Hey!" she said. "I waited at our table for *ages*." She looked around. "You're the one always banging on about me not going out to get raped and murdered."

Then she looked at me, really *looked* at me. Shit. Shit. She reached down and touched my face, and I closed my eyes. I held her hand there and she said, "Hey."

I pushed her, and she pushed me back and we were laughing and then, and then she leaned in and we were kissing, and she was laughing again.

"You should see your face!" She leaned in and we were kissing again.

I nudged her away, and I was trying to tell her. And she gave me a look and said, "Shut up, Will. Like I don't know."

How much would Alex hate me if she knew I was a Breeder runner all those months we were together? If she knew about all those innocent kids I put away?

•

This is what I want. I want to be in the water with you. It's October and the water's late warmth presses against us. We're on boards, facing the ocean. The ocean, the ocean. There's a wave coming.

We talked about it—how in a different world, where the oceans weren't burnt, the lands weren't barren, where we could walk around freely, it might happen. In that world, two girls are walking down a beach, hand-in-hand, laughing. They're walking under a clear blue sky, breathing clean air, and they have their whole lives ahead of them. They can swim and surf all day, their skin growing hot under the sun. They can smell the fresh salt in the air and they watch the men and women throwing lines on the shore, catching fat rainbow fish. The girls will buy one of those fish and cook it on a fire under the stars.

Is there a world out there, beyond the badlands, where this is possible? If Alex is right, and the Response has made contact with other cities, maybe there is still a place like this, somewhere. Or maybe we could work to build one. In another world, we'd have our lives ahead of us. We'd have choices. We'd be able to hold hands and walk into that future together.

But not in this world.

●

I'm woken in the night by an orange suit who hands me a mobile phone, some tape, and some pieces of elastic. He says, "You can do what you need to do now—our man is watching." He nods at the camera. "Cate's moved cells again."

"How will I get the package from the surgeon's?"

"We have someone on her staff. They'll make contact once you're there."

I take off my hoodie and use the tape and elastic to set up small pockets, close to my body, then put the hoodie back on. The orange suit nods and leaves.

I watch the phone all night. At dawn it lights up and I answer it.

"I've found out about your grandmother. Jessica Meadows is deceased. I'm so sorry, Will."

I've always known that they would have killed Ma right away, but I feel sudden pain all over. It's real—she's gone. And her death is on me. I think back to that morning. I should have gone home straight after meeting Alex in the diner. Ma must've been so worried that day—not knowing anything, wondering where I was. And then she would have heard the choppers coming. First, in the distance—and then, closer. The slow realization that they were coming for her. And Alex—if only I'd talked her down that day, if only I'd convinced her to walk home instead, to stay in the Gray Zone. I see myself on that bus, setting everything in motion, and I can hardly breathe.

"Your grandmother's original name was Sophie Gray," Cate continues. "She was a member of the Response."

"No, I don't think that's right. You must have another Jessica Meadows."

"That's what my contacts say. They're usually correct."

"What does that mean, Cate? That she was member of the Response?"

"She joined when she was in the Incubator—that's when most join. My contacts say she worked hard from inside. That she was instrumental in helping some of the younger ones escape. After she was released, she continued to help the Response with intelligence and with resources, when she could. She even hid our people when needed. But around ten years ago, she said she had to stop contact with us, that she wasn't in a safe place any longer."

I think of the people we kept hidden in the first house I remember, the house carved into the wall. We didn't hide people after we moved. She chose me over her work with the Response.

"Do you know how she died?"

"The Rator, Will. I'm sorry."

"Was she interrogated?"

She pauses. "She was. I'm so sorry to tell you. Are you alright?"

"Yeah." Ma was such a brave person, and spent her final moments in pain and terror. She deserved so much more. And it's all on me.

"I've heard you'll be taken to Zone A today. Don't forget our agreement."

"All good."

"This phone is a burner—give it back to an orange suit now, will you?"

"Roger that."

Moments later, the sliding door to my cell opens and I hand over the phone.

•

I'm sedated, put in another Incubator van, and taken away that morning, just as Cate said I would be. When I open my eyes, there's the warm light again. Daylight is coming into the room from all directions. There are big, open windows with a gentle breeze coming straight through. The air is so fresh and sharp, it could cut you. No mask; I feel it touching my skin. I think of the dome over Zone A—we could always see it glittering, reflecting in the sun, but I never imagined it would feel like *this*. The air carries scents from the outside world: dirt, petrol, fresh-mown grass. I try to name them and I feel giddy with the stimulus. My god—I can smell *coffee*.

The painted angels are there, above me—I'm in the surgeon's long room, the one with the soft bed, the same room as last time. I concentrate on an angel in the center: gazing up, ecstatic. I hope Ma has found her Heaven. I hope Ma has her own angel who protects her and makes her happy.

Outside, a bird calls.

No shackles, no drip. I'm on a gurney. There are bandages on the left side of my face. There's a fresh pot of coffee and some pastries on a tray to the side of my bed.

The surgeon is sitting next to me in a large, wooden chair, holding out a small plate with a croissant on it. I'm not sure how afraid I should be. I take the croissant and bite into it, and she pours me a cup of coffee. She holds it out, and I take that too and drink. I try not to show how good it is. I take another sip. I'm back in Zone A, and for the first time I can remember, I'm not physically suffering. That in itself is enough to make me feel high. I feel like myself again. At the same time, I don't know what it means to be myself—or at least, who I was before I was broken down. The pain and loneliness have made me into something else.

I raise a hand to my face and feel the bandages crinkle.

"I've had your Breeder brand removed," she says. "It will feel tender for some weeks. There'll be no permanent mark."

"Why?"

"You have a beautiful face," she says, ignoring my question. She reaches over and touches my jaw

I flinch—both at the word *beautiful* and at her touch.

"Handsome, then," she says. The surgeon hands me a mirror and my sad reflection looks back at me. The softness of my face; the curls of hair that frame it. Well-fed, healthy skin. It's not me. I put the mirror down.

"I want to live as a boy again," I say, so quietly I doubt she'll hear To be honest, I've never exactly felt like a boy, but I sure as hell don't feel like a Breeder. I wish I didn't have to be either. I wish I could just float above all this, without a body at all. Or without a body that had to be one particular thing. But if I have to choose—and it seems I have to—then I'll live as a boy. Living as a Breeder is no life for anyone.

"That simply isn't possible," says the surgeon.

I turn and look her full in the face. "What do you want from me?"

"Ah, that Westie bluntness again!" She holds my gaze. "Except, you're not really a Westie. Are you?"

"What are you talking about?"

"We do genetic profiles on all Breeders when they arrive at the Incubator, Will," she says. "You're one hundred percent Corporation. There's no Westie in you at all."

"That's bullshit!" I tell her. I belong to Ma. In my mind, all I can see is Ma, and Cranky, and our little home in Zone F. I'm as Westie as they come.

She shakes her head. "I was able to link your genetic tests to our records." She holds up her phone, shows me a photo of a young girl.

"This was your Breeder. We have her records on file."

I reach out to touch the phone. I can't stop myself. The surgeon lets me. The photo is of a girl about thirteen years old—it must have been taken soon after they put her in the Incubator. She is small for her age, and she is unsmiling, look-ing up defiantly at whoever is taking the photo. I gently trace her outline with my finger.

"Not my Breeder. My *mother*."

"She's not your mother, Will. Breeders are only surrogates for Corp babies. Of course the Corp wants all the babies' genes to be Corp. Didn't you know that?" She's genuinely surprised that I don't know.

I shake my head. I feel dizzy and stupid.

"I mean. If we wanted Westie genes we'd just open up the Wall. Millions of people waiting out there!" She laughs.

This is *not* what the Corp tells us. Only 5 percent of people are fertile, so I know most Breeders are surrogates, but the Corp tells us that the babies birthed at the Incubator are genet-ically both Corp *and* Westie. That the Corp is desperate to make the most of what fertility is left, to guarantee the future of the human species. Did Ma know I wasn't her genetic grandkid?

If Ma was part of the Response, she must have known that all Incubator babies are Corp. If so, why would Ma look after a Corp kid? She kept so much from me.

My mother escaped from the Incubator, where she was incubating a Corp baby—me. I never belonged to my mother, and I never belonged to Ma. Ma must have known that. And yet she kept me. I feel like I'm losing Ma all over again—there's pain deep in my core. What was Ma thinking? She gave up every-thing for me, a Corp bastard. Why didn't she just give me back to them? As a member of the Response, surely a part of her must have wanted me as far away from her as possible?

"Does it say how my mother escaped the Incubator?" I ask the surgeon.

"Your Breeder escaped as part of a suicide mission with the Response, but then defected from her group. Presumably to have you."

A suicide mission? "That's not what I was told."

She shrugs. "That's what her security record states."

Yet again, I think about who I should trust and who I should believe.

The surgeon swipes to two more photos.

"These are your Corp bio parents. You look like your bio mother, don't you? You have the same eyes."

I look a *lot* like her. But seeing her, I feel nothing.

Ma loved me so much and I loved her, and she knew I was her Corp enemy—genetically, at least. It doesn't make sense. She sent me out, beyond the Wall, to capture her own people, so I could buy the drugs that kept me safe—that doesn't make sense either. *Just survive, Will, and try to be happy. That's all there is.*

"I'm not a Breeder," I say.

"Well, actually, *legally*, you are. Legally, you're still bound to the Incubator. But only until your new contract."

She holds up her phone. There's a picture of a baby. I turn away.

"Don't do that. She's your ticket out of here."

She smiles. "Have I got your attention?"

She has.

"You know of course, Will, that Corp girls—Zone A girls—don't go into the Incubator?"

"No," I say. According to what we learned at school, it's important that every zone contributes. I mean, I know that Breeder Incubations are a key way for Westies to assimilate into the Corporation. But I was told that Corp Breeders were Incubated too.

"Do you know what happens to the babies who are born in the Incubator?"

"They're taken to Zone C, initially," I tell her. "Then they're assessed and plugged into the system—allocated a zone, given their initial unit allocation, and evaluated continuously from there." From birth to death, and so on, forever.

The surgeon smirks at me. "Where'd you hear *that*?"

"School."

"You really don't know the truth?"

I shrug, embarrassed and confused.

"We only adopt them out to Corp people. Strictly Zone A. For a very high price. It's our mission to preserve our genetic connection to the original Corp families. The Incubator was built to serve them. Us."

She holds up a photo of a baby—my baby. "And your kid is

fully Corp. You weren't just a surrogate—we used your egg. I needed to see if your eggs were viable after all your chemical exposure in the outer zones. And they are. Do you know how valuable *that* makes you?"

I look at the photo. It's the first time I've seen the baby properly. Her. She's small and red and angry. I'm glad she looks so angry. Seeing her little face makes me feel strange—angry too, but something else. Before I can think too much more about her, the surgeon swipes to the next photo: two good-looking, middle-aged women.

"Your daughter belongs to them now, Will. They're both Corp lawyers. They're delighted to have her. More important, they've paid a significant fee for her."

It's surreal to think that—she—was in my body. I can't think of it—her—as mine. But more than that, I can't bear the fact that I brought her into this hell.

"Will she be a Breeder?" I ask.

"No. No, she will never be a Breeder. I keep telling you— only Westies are Breeders. The Corporation only has women and girls. She'll have a wonderful life with more than she could dream of. Don't give her another thought."

"So is everyone in Zone A rich?" I ask.

"No," she says. "We have rich and poor."

"But—what about the outer zones? They're part of the Corporation too."

"Well, yes. Technically. But they're not part of Zone A." She smiles. "I mean, we need the other zones for labor and reproduction. But Westies are excluded from Zone A. We don't want them as part of our actual lives, do we?"

We? "So—what do you want from me?" I ask her again.

"I want to take you out of the Incubator."

"You want to . . . adopt me?"

She laughs. "No, you little idiot. I want to *lease* you to a college. Or rather—lease your valuable genetic assets. Keep our Corp bloodlines going."

I don't get it. "Lease me for what?"

She smiles.

"I'll kill myself rather than be pregnant again," I say. "You know I'll do it."

"College girls aren't Breeders," she says.

•

I'm sitting on a swivel chair in the middle of the surgeon's room. Behind me, a short man is styling my long, curly brown hair with an ironing device and some sweet-smelling spray. The surgeon sits beside me, talking about the college system and my future role in it. I force myself to stay calm. I need to find an angle.

When the stylist finishes, my hair looks pretty much exactly as it did thirty minutes ago, but he and the surgeon both smile and sigh appreciatively before he leaves.

The surgeon shows in another man, who gently peels the bandage off my face. I can see a faint shadow of the Breeder mark and I go to touch it, but the man gently presses my hand down. He takes out some tiny containers and applies ointment, which instantly cools the skin. He then puts concealer over the mark, dabbing and blending. Soon, he's applying bright colors all over my face.

The surgeon throws some clothes onto the table in front

of me. "Different styles you can choose from," she says. "Now, I know you've been living as a boy for a long time . . ."

I can't look her in the eye. I pick through the clothes. They're exquisite, made of soft fabric with sharp corners, but all are, definitely, dresses. Their colors are bold, so different from the muted tones we wear in the outer zones, and some of the collars and cuffs have actual jewels sewn into them.

"It would be more profitable for you to present as a girl as we negotiate the contract. And for the next few years. College girls on your kind of scholarship *do* tend to present as very feminine. For the purposes of maximizing bonuses and such. It's a marketing thing. Okay?"

"Okay," I say. I don't want to talk about my body at all.

"Great! Anyway, Corp males and females are completely equal," she says.

"I'm sure that's totally the case," I say, and reach for the most androgynous-looking dress in the pile.

"Right!" she agrees, because apparently they don't have sarcasm in Zone A.

"What about my bio parents?" I ask the surgeon, sweetly. "Won't they want to know about me?" I imagine contacting them out of the blue, their long-lost Corp kid, ready to emerge full-grown into their lives and be cared for and loved. Ready for me to work them, to escape.

She smiles sweetly back at me. "You're one of two hundred fifty-three offspring for your bio mother," she says. "For your bio father, it's four times that number. Like me, they're rare super-producers—I have three hundred fifty-two genetic offspring, myself—and, like me, I imagine they haven't given a thought to you beyond the big unit reward they got from the

Corp, fifteen years ago, when you showed up in their accounts as a live birth. They honestly wouldn't give a shit."

I go into the restroom and change from my tracksuit into the dress. There's a mirror, and through the bright makeup, I see my face has some of its angles and lines back, because I'm no longer on Breeder hormones. Though it's still rounder than it was when I was on Crystal. All thanks to those nutritional, terrible-tasting cubes of mush. I want to smash the fucking mirror.

I walk out and the surgeon says, "Game time," and as we start to walk down the hall, she puts her hand on the small of my back as though she's scared I'll run off. I can tell she's anxious and since I'm not used to seeing any emotion in her, this makes me interested.

We go past a large, circular staircase in the middle of the house and I look up, hoping to see what's above. I count five floors. There are corridors leading out in four directions. I can't believe this is a place where just one person lives. The surgeon seems to have a full staff.

A door slams and there are footsteps coming down the staircase toward us. A young woman, a little older than me, freezes when she sees us. She meets my eye and I look back directly, in case she's my contact for Cate. But the expression she shoots back takes me by surprise—fury. Then she quickly looks away and asks the surgeon something about wine glasses.

●

I'm sitting at the surgeon's dining table in an enormous room. In front of me is a sheet of heavy paper titled *Luncheon*, with over twenty menu items. There's proper linen, a bottle of wine, and candles. The surgeon and another guest sit at the table, and they each have two attendants on either side of them—two beautiful young people, who are not waitstaff, but who are just standing there, decoratively, wearing the dresses I saw earlier, as well as jewelry in their ears and on their necks and wrists. At the top of the room are more young people, their faces, sad, holding the musical instruments I've heard. I don't know the names of all of them, but I know the large one is a cello, and the small one a violin. There's a piano. And then wind instruments—so many.

"Please help yourselves," the surgeon says, as waitstaff bring platters of meat and vegetables and fish to the table. It makes my eyes water—there's enough to feed a family for several weeks—and it just keeps coming. The surgeon has made all her staff wear a uniform. I watch them glance at her when she isn't looking and they clearly hate her guts. They may be Corporation and live in Zone A, but in this respect they're just like us Westies—they can't do anything about it.

Opposite me sits an older man, the dean of Excelsior College, which the surgeon says is the most prestigious college in Zone A.

"Your aunt tells me you're planning to apply for college this year," says the dean. He says the word *aunt* in scare quotes— "aunt"—which tells me that the dean is "in on it," although I'm not yet clear what *it* is. And I'm sure that, just like in the Gray Zone, both the surgeon and the dean have different interests in *it*, and different leverage to get what they want.

"Yes," I say, as I to try to read the situation.

"She also tells me you're a super-producer," the dean continues.

I look at the surgeon, who nods. "I was telling the dean earlier that we've tested your ovaries. Based on your egg count and egg quality, as well as the fertility history of your bio-parents and the quality of your live birth, I have no doubt that you're a super-producer. Increasingly rare. And valuable." She takes a sip of wine.

I feel a shiver up my spine. It's not as though I'm used to privacy or anything, but it would be great if I could get through one day without someone mentioning my body or its "outputs."

"I sincerely hope you're considering Excelsior," the dean says. I look at the surgeon, who raises her eyebrows slightly.

"Yes," I tell the dean. "I'm considering a couple of places, but Excelsior is definitely up there."

The surgeon smiles. The dean stops smiling. "Do you think you'll major in the sciences or the humanities?"

"Science, I think."

"Contributing to the collective good," he opines. "That's wonderful. There's so much work to be done in infertility, human health . . ." he trails off. "Does she actually understand the college system?" he whispers to the surgeon. So he must know I'm not the surgeon's niece. I wonder how much he's getting paid, and how.

The surgeon shrugs, turns to me. "This is how it works. Super-producers like you are allowed to attend elite Zone A colleges for four years. They get a superior education, they live a superior life. All they have to do is provide the Corp with gametes. It's easier for the boys, of course, but they have to play their part too." The dean smiles at her. "The girls go on fertility drugs every sixty days. They have their eggs extracted—we can get up to forty or fifty eggs each time. We create embryos, test them for problems, and put the viable embryos into Breeders. Right now, with super-producers like you, we're getting forty pregnancies every two months."

The dean interrupts. "Is it really that high?"

"Yes," she says to the dean. "Ever since we implemented embryo testing."

She turns back to me. "Now, the kids who are infertile, or less fertile, they're not getting the same privileges you are—unless they're very, very wealthy and their families can pay the tuition themselves. Every Corp kid is forced by law to give us their gametes, if they're fertile, but they're unlikely to secure a place at an elite college unless they're a super-producer. There are lots of lower-tier colleges out there for the others. The musicians here tonight are from a local musical college, working off some of their debt. Does all that make sense?"

"Yes," I say, my mind racing. I turn to the dean. "I'd like to study genetics." I can feel my face grow hot, being so open, but it's true—I'd love to research ways to get beyond infertility. A Westie kid studying genetics at an elite university. What would Ma say?

"Splendid," says the dean.

Then the door opens, and a member of staff shows somebody else in.

"Sorry I'm late!" the new person says. He's a middle-aged, Rob-style man. The surgeon introduces him as "Luke Stone, a college admissions agent," but he is clearly a Gray Corps affiliate. A kid like me who's grown up in Zone F will always know who's in the Gray Corps, who's Corp, who's Westie; how to read them and what they really want and how to play them. As soon as I see that the Gray Corps is involved, everything becomes clear. While recruitment of fertile kids to colleges seems to be part of Zone A life and is legal, I'm sure poaching Breeders from the Incubator is not—or rather, recruitment under the table for a huge unit bonus is not. Just as Ma always said, the whole world runs on dirty money and the ruddy-faced, proper-looking dean is "laundering" me and my eggs through his college as though I were a real Corp girl from Zone A. The only way he can do that is with the help of the Gray Corps, so that means Luke. Luke's handling the transfer of units, and my new ID in the Grid. And he's not only handling the setup of the deal—he's going to be laundering each new egg production.

The dean smiles at Luke, not looking bothered by his presence at all, which confirms my hunch.

"I'm so glad we're all here now," the dean says. He sits up, clearly getting ready to make a speech. "You know, I've always been so proud of Excelsior College and my work there. I know you're considering offers from other schools . . ." he nods to me and Luke hides his surprise well. "So I'll outline what I think we can offer you at Excelsior. As your aunt has probably told you, my college consistently ranks number one in the zone. We are the oldest college and, in fact, we predate the End Times, having served the original Corporation families long before the Fourth World Depression."

The dean likes to hear his own voice, and he has a great sense of his own importance. The surgeon calls over another waitstaff to fill the dean's glass.

"We pride ourselves on welcoming our scholarship students—the super donors—at Excelsior as warmly as we welcome the Corp's oldest and finest families," he says. "So, madam, I would like to raise a toast to yourself and your *niece*."

He holds up his glass. I look over at the surgeon and see that she's holding her glass up too, and so is Luke, so I hold mine up, even though I've already drunk whatever was in it.

"Let's talk specific terms," Luke says, with some impatience.

The dean clears his throat and the look on his and the surgeon's face almost makes me laugh. They're obviously not used to dealing with Gray Corps affiliates, who prefer to talk bluntly. The surgeon and the dean would both rather pretend that this is an elegant social dinner, not a corrupt meeting where they're leasing out a fifteen-year-old's eggs. As they talk, I steal glances at Luke. After so long in the Incubator, I stare at Luke more than I should, because I find him weirdly soothing—a reminder of my old life.

The dean looks meaningfully at me. "Shall we retire to another room?"

Luke shrugs. "She may as well hear terms." I'm the object of the contract and there's nothing I can do about the terms anyway—If I take a step wrong, Luke and his Gray Corps affiliates will stick me in the Rator. I pretend to be fascinated by my food and the fizzy drink that makes me light-headed, but I pay careful attention to all the details. The sums are unreal—one hundred thousand units each to the dean, the surgeon, and Luke on signing; but the real kicker is *twenty thousand to each, for every live birth*. At 240 births per year that's almost five million units per year. Each. The initial one hundred thousand units will come from a Corporation endowment, the dean says, which means the dean will be laundering me under the auspices of a "special scholarship," paid for by his college. The five-million-unit live-birth payments will be paid for by the new parents, directly to the college. A waitstaff refills my glass and when she puts it back on the table, she leaves her hand around it a second too long. She doesn't look at me. She turns and before she walks away, hesitates. Then I hear her feet moving quickly along the carpet.

"Can I go to the bathroom?" I ask the surgeon.

She nods. "Of course."

I head outside the room as fast as I can without being too obvious, but the corridor is empty. I walk down until I get to the central staircase. I can hear footsteps running up the top of the stairs, but I can't see anyone. Then I turn and enter the bathroom. I'm only there a few seconds when there's a sharp knock. I open the door and there she is: she's my age, dressed in the uniform, and holding out a package the size of an egg.

"For Cate," she says, pushing her way inside the bathroom with me. "Long live the Response."

"Thanks," I say. I work quickly to take the package apart. It contains basic materials that are banned everywhere. She watches as I hide the components in my underwear and bra and inside the small pockets I've made from tape and elastic and then I give her back the plastic container.

There's hostility in her look. "What?" I say.

"Were you really a Breeder?" she asks.

I nod.

"And now they're working out how to send you to Excelsior?" she asks. "Well, good luck, then," she says sarcastically and leaves.

I count to five, flush the toilet and come out. But she's already gone.

Back in the overheated room, the three people around the table are scanning each other's chips, transferring holding deposits.

•

The dean graciously condescends to shake my hand before he leaves.

"Trinity term has just ended," he says, a little drunkenly, "so we'll have you start in Michaelmas term. But why don't you start coming into the college over the vacation so you can familiarize yourself with the library and the labs? I'll get a couple of my favorite students to show you around."

He's flushed with the booze and his win. "I am so very pleased you will be joining us at Excelsior," he goes on. "In fact, why don't you join us tomorrow for our end of term celebrations? I'll arrange a temporary pass for you, Will."

"That would be so lovely," says the surgeon, and they shake hands. "We would *adore* that."

•

After they've left, the surgeon is glowing. A member of staff gives me my Incubator tracksuit and I change in the bathroom. Then the surgeon places her hand on the small of my back again, walking me toward the foyer. I'm very conscious of the explosive components tucked around my body, and how close they are to her hand, as she says, "I'm going to explain how the contract between you and I will work. Nothing official, of course, but I'll uphold my end. Do you understand?"

I nod.

Then she lays it all out. I will become a college girl and serve my four years. "You'll live with me while I teach you how to be a college girl. You'll need a new name, Will, and a new history. You must never tell anyone you were a Westie, or a Breeder. Everything is conditional on your ongoing performance under the contract. I can send you back to the Incubator any time.

"I'll pay you ten thousand units upfront. After the four years, if you hit all your contractual points—generate two hundred forty live births per year—I will pay you an additional fifty thousand units. Then you'll be released into Zone B with a profesh job. You'll be able to put down a deposit on a house, Will. You'll be able to save some of your own gametes at the Incubator and use Corp sperm to make future children."

A year ago, this was my dream. Now, I couldn't care less, unless Alex can come too.

"I agree to your terms," I tell her. "But . . ." I hesitate—you can make a threat or a demand to someone exactly *once.*

"Yes?"

"I have a . . . condition."

"A *condition*? You mean, apart from me not sending you to the Incubator for the next twenty years?"

Has she forgotten that I've heard the sums involved? She's not going to give me up. I talk quickly, to get it all out. "When I was put in the Incubator, my girlfriend Alex was too. I want her to be released as part of my contract. I want her to stop breeding immediately and go to work with the kids in the Preincubation Program at the same time that I go to college. Then, when I've finished my contract, I want her to come with me, into Zone B. With her own profesh job, and her own units."

The surgeon looks genuinely surprised. I can tell she's never heard of Alex, and she's usually so on top of her data. We're standing in the middle of the foyer and she types into her device, bringing up Alex's file. I can see a young photo of Alex, probably from her last Incubation. She flicks through the record.

"I don't see what you're actually offering me here," the surgeon says, looking at me with her clear, impassive eyes.

I feel a shot of anger, as I literally could give her nothing more, considering that she's leasing my full person for the next four years. But I know it's nothing personal. To the Corp, every single person is a contractual opportunity.

"Honestly?" I say. "I'm wondering how I'll survive the next four years—and how you'll get your five million units a year—without killing myself. Unless I can see a point to it all. For me, Alex would be that point."

She considers, then nods. "I'll have to look into it. Especially into Alex. Of course, I'd want you to increase your output—we'd add four more egg retrievals each year that would go entirely to me."

"Okay."

"But this is not settled yet, do you understand? I'm just agreeing to look into it."

"Yes. Okay. Thank you."

I'm smiling, despite myself. I can hardly breathe, I'm so happy.

She hands me a small, pretty box. "Here's a new cell device for you. Everyone will have one tomorrow at the college. And I want us to be able to stay in touch."

"Thanks," I say and take it out. It's bright red and sleek.

"It's set up so you can only contact me or Luke on it," she adds.

When we step outside, Luke is waiting for us. He has changed into an orange suit.

The surgeon smiles at him. "Luke has been agreed upon by all parties to protect you. Now that your contract is in process, everyone wants to preserve their asset. Of course, as soon as Luke's people organize your new chip and your transfer to Zone A on the Grid, we'll move you up to Zone A permanently," she says.

Luke and I nod at each other, like we're regular people, like he's not my personal prison guard.

"Let's go," Luke says, and I follow him to the garage.

I see that Luke's car is crap—just a run-down, silver sedan. I'm quick to hide my surprise. Luke's car tells me that he's relatively low down in the Gray Corps, which in turn tells me that he wasn't once a legit Corp who went crooked—like Corp lawyer Rob—but that he's a Westie like me, who has to move slowly, painstakingly, through the Gray Corps ranks.

We drive away from the surgeon's house. It's late afternoon and it's the first time I've been in Zone A without being in the back of an Incubator van, sedated. I see the surgeon's house from outside: a six-story, red-stone mansion. We pass similar houses and drive down similar streets and I think about how in each of those houses, there's only one person, or perhaps a family, kept there by a full staff. I think about the crowded apartment blocks in Zone F, where two or three families might live, of the shacks Ma and I lived in. Here, there are parks and so many beautiful trees. We slow at some traffic lights and I see two people waiting to cross the road.

"What's wrong with their skin?" I ask Luke. "What disease is that?"

He looks over. "No disease," he says. "They're just old."

"How old?"

"Eighty? Maybe eighty-five?"

I must have gasped because he nods. "It's true."

I can't think of anyone I know who's older than fifty, maybe sixty tops. It gets harder and harder to keep up with the Corp rates of productivity as you get older, so a lot of old people get taken out during the Rator Days.

Then the city changes and the buildings get denser—there are lots of smaller houses, and then apartment buildings. By the time we reach the security post to Zone B, we're passing high-rise buildings and offices. This is where the less privileged people of Zone A live. They're still nice places, but there's a vast difference between these apartment blocks and the surgeon's house.

As we approach the Incubator, I watch Luke's face in the rearview mirror, as I used to do with Rob. I'm trying to place Luke: shitty car, probably thirty-five years old. He's only a low-level Gray Corps affiliate, and that means he has years of this sad life ahead of him. So maybe he'd take a risk to go up the ranks quickly. It's a tricky business, reading people.

Luke stares at the road ahead and doesn't meet my eyes once. When we get to the Incubator, he holds his wrist to the scanner, and the gates open—the surgeon has obviously sorted his ID. We park and he's nodded through the front door and walks up to my cell with me. Now I'm wondering how the hell I'm going to get the package to Cate, so I can see Alex, with Luke hanging around.

•

In the middle of the night, I'm shaken awake and I look up and see an orange Shadow suit holding a flashlight. Luke is immediately awake, and the Shadow jumps back—clearly shocked to see an orange suit in my cell at this hour who isn't one of Cate's—but she recovers quickly.

"I'm on special duty with this Breeder," Luke says, and the Shadow scans his wrist and nods, seeing that he has the authority of the surgeon.

"I need to take her for a random drug test," she says, shackling my wrist to hers. "Illegal trade is up."

Luke nods, and starts to walk toward the sliding doors with us, when the suit shakes her head. "No, you can't attend. The Code states that only Shadow guards can accompany Breeders to medical. Remember?"

Luke nods.

"We'll be back in fifteen minutes."

Luke hesitates, realizes he doesn't have a comeback, and then says, "Okay."

She takes me into the corridor, and with my free hand, I double-check that the components are still in the pockets under my tracksuit.

It's so strange to be walking around the Incubator at night. I can see the clear doors all around the Circle, lit by the low night lights. Only a couple of doors have figures behind them, staring out. I look away, so as not to make eye contact or to attract attention. The orange suit is silent, leading me by the wrist to the end of the corridor, down the fire escape and down, down, down six flights of metal stairs. I'm slow and puffing because I'm not used to the exercise. She tugs my wrist. "Hurry up."

At the bottom, she swings open the heavy door and hands me a face mask and then pushes me outside. "I'll be right here," she says, leaning against the fire exit and taking out a pack of cigarettes.

I put my mask on and start stamping the ground from the cold and blowing into my cupped hands. It's one of those rare, forty-degree nights. I'm not used to the mask anymore and it makes my face itchy, so I take it off, then start wheezing, and put it back on. I unzip my tracksuit and start to rip out the components. I'm looking up at the camera and cursing how long it's taking Cate to show up. Then I hear footsteps and a voice.

"Will?" It's *Alex.*

She's come around the corner with another orange suit, who leaves us to it and moves to the stairwell. Now Alex is standing in front of me. Her bright eyes, her beautiful face. I tear my mask off.

I move forward to hug her, but she backs away, wraps her arms around her body. I get it. After everything that's happened, I don't want another human touching me again either. Ever. Except Alex. She looks so different—so pale, and her eyes are bright with pain and anger, not her old joy.

"Cate sent me for the components," she says.

I hold out my hand and Alex takes them and nods and now she smiles, and I see the old Alex again. She puts everything in her pockets and looks at me with her big, frank eyes. How strange I must look to her: my fat, pink cheeks, my long, curly hair. Almost unrecognizable.

"Will," she says. "They told me you tried to kill yourself."

"Yeah."

She takes both my hands in hers. "It's okay," she says. "It's okay, Will."

It's so good to hear her voice, to feel her touch. I'm suddenly filled with ridiculous hope. What if the surgeon agrees to my terms and Alex and I get to have a life one day? What if?

"Listen, Will," she says, looking around to where her guard is standing with mine, about thirty feet away, both smoking and talking. Then she clasps my hands more tightly, and starts talking quickly about the Response, and about their plans for a new world.

I put my hand on her arm to stop her. She flinches. "Alex, do you know what those parts are for?"

She nods, her eyes bright. "Cate's going to blow up the

Incubator, destroy key infrastructure. The Night of Fires. I've volunteered. I want you to as well, Will. You know how to work systems. Cate . . . doesn't think we can trust you, but I told her we can. You could help us so much."

I suck in my breath. "A suicide mission?"

Alex nods.

"I mean . . . I get it. If they're going to drive us to suicide, we should take them with us on the way out. I'm not afraid to die."

"Right!" Alex says, smiling. "The Corp was built by people like us. Literally, by our blood and our flesh. It's time for us to take it over."

I think of the Book Shadow, the courtroom with the weeping Shadows, Rob pushing the Shadows into the Rator. "It's pointless," I say gently. "You know how it goes—the Corp always crushes the Response."

Alex looks at me, angry. "Every act of resistance matters. I don't care if it takes generations . . . it starts with us."

"The Corp will kill you, Alex." I can hear my voice, high and panicky, when what I want is to stay calm and to reason with her carefully.

"So? I'll die blowing up part of the Incubator. And more girls will come after us and die blowing up other pieces. We'll do it slowly. I don't care! I'd rather die fighting those fuckers than live like this."

She pulls me closer, holds my hands to her lips. "Say yes! I told Cate you would!"

There are tears in my eyes. I can't stand the thought of anything happening to her. I look over at the orange suits. They're halfway through their cigarettes. We don't have much time—I have to just go for it.

"Alex, what if I could get us out of here?"

Alex stares at me. "What are you talking about?"

"Have you heard from Cate that I've been taken to Zone A?"

Her face is closed, unreadable. "Yes."

"Listen . . . this is going to sound nuts, but I have a direct connection with the chief surgeon of the Incubator. I have a *deal* with her to get us both out of here. We have a shot at real lives. Out of the Incubator into Zone B, with jobs and a house and everything."

She laughs. "A deal with the *Corp*? How?"

"It's complicated." I can feel my face getting hot. Will Alex work out that I'm really a Corp?

"Will. Tell me how."

I ignore her question. "I said yes to their deal. But only if they take both of us out of the Incubator."

Alex's face is full of horror. "No, Will. *No*."

"Alex, think about it. An actual *life*, instead of years in the Incubator. Being happy. In Zone B!"

"You mean, live a great life while everyone here suffers and dies? No way. That's so *fucked*, Will."

"Listen though. We could still help the Response. From the inside, from Zone B. From a place of strength. We would find out about how everything really works. I mean, who knows what we could do? Has anyone from the Response even done that before? And we could do it *together*. We could fight the Corp together."

"No," Alex says. "What you're talking about is *complicity*."

"Alex, I swear! I can think of scenarios where I'd strap a suicide vest on and head to the barricades but not when there's a chance at life. We have a chance, Alex!"

"That's . . . it's evil, Will."

My heart's racing. This is going much worse than I thought it would.

"It's time to pick a side, Will."

We stare at each other. I want to bring back the old Alex before it's time to go. I feel annihilated. She's never going to change her mind. I look over at the orange suits. They've finished their cigarettes and look like they're readying to get back. "When's the Night of Fires?" I ask.

She looks away from me. I feel that distrust again. "Alex?"

"Night after tomorrow," she says. "Don't tell her I told you."

"Are you sure we can trust *her*?"

She nods without hesitation and I feel a pang. "With all my heart. I knew her when I was in the Incubator last time—before she was leader. Cate got me out of here back then—she set off a bomb that freed a bunch of the youngest Breeders, including me. I owe her everything."

I sigh.

"Will, long before I knew you, I was part of the Response. It's my whole life."

"Okay. I get it."

She nods. "Cate said something else . . ." She takes a step away from me, pulls her arms tight around herself, her whole body tense.

"What is it?"

She looks away, then starts talking quickly. "Cate said that she found out you were a Breeder runner. I told her that's bullshit. I told her there was no way in hell. It's bullshit, isn't it?"

Fuck. Alex looks up at me. For a second, I think of lying to her, just because I can't stand the thought of what's coming next. But I can't.

"Cate's right, but . . ."

I step toward her, my hand outreached, but she pushes me away and starts to cry.

"Alex?" She doesn't answer. "Alex?"

"I can't believe you could do that," she says, so softly I can barely hear her. "And I can't believe you lied about it."

I just stand there, my heart banging. There's nothing more to say about it.

"At least promise me you won't have anything more to do with this deal," she says.

"But, Alex, it's our only chance . . ."

"Promise me!"

I hesitate. "I can't promise, Alex. I just can't."

The orange suits move toward us. Alex looks at me and then leans in and whispers—"Long live the Response!"—as the orange suits separate us and take us back to our cells.

•

I spend the night wide awake, my jaw clenched. As much as I want to live, and as much as I want a life which has Alex In it— even if it's just knowing she's in the world somewhere—every time I think back to her face, I know that she'll never, ever change her mind. She'll never, ever compromise. She'll never let me take her to Zone B. I can't drag her out of the Incubator only to imprison her another way.

I may as well strap a bomb to myself. I may as well tell Cate yes. *Yes, Cate, I'll run bombs for you, even though I know the surgeon and all her cronies will shut the Response down and send us all to the Rator and our deaths won't change a thing.*

My mind ticks over, trying to think of some other way out, and keeps coming up with nothing.

In the morning, Luke and I drive to the surgeon's house in Zone A. When I arrive, the surgeon gives me another fancy dress to change into, and then Luke escorts me to the passenger seat of the surgeon's black sports car. The surgeon hands me a giant, delicious-smelling coffee in a large cup with a Latin insignia plastered on it. I wrap my hands around it.

"Remember that you're my niece," the surgeon says, as I fidget in the passenger seat next to her. "You've transferred from Astor College in the north of Zone A. Alright?"

"Yep." The surgeon is taking me to Excelsior College. It's a special celebration day or something, and the surgeon is beside herself. She went to Excelsior herself and she can't wait to see it again.

"Stop fidgeting!" she says, and I stop playing with the remote buttons for the windows.

"I'll introduce you to some other college girls," she continues. "It's important that you make a good impression."

"Okay."

We drive in silence for a few minutes, and then the surgeon pulls her sports car up to the Excelsior College security post. I try to look past it, into the college grounds. Excelsior College was apparently part of the original city, the one that stood before the End Times. A lot of it was razed to the ground but they rebuilt it, and the bones of some of the original buildings remain today. This is where the country's richest families have studied for hundreds of years.

The surgeon is holding her coffee in a gloved hand as she talks to the CSO, who then waves us through. The tall metal gates open and we drive down a long, smooth, straight road.

As we drive, the surgeon proudly points out the key landmarks.

"The Flatiron building, as they had in New York," she says. "A famous city from Before. We were able to source the correct bricks."

"The Cathedral of Notre Dame," she says, as we drive past a giant stone church.

"The Sydney Harbor Bridge," as we drive over an actual goddamn bridge. I'm looking at the surgeon with my eyebrows raised but she doesn't even register. "Excelsior College campus has reproduced the best parts of cities from the old world."

"That's nice," I say.

"We also have a Versailles, including genuine reproductions of its key treasures, but it's on the other side of campus," she says, in an apologetic tone.

We're meant to be in a state of emergency, yet the Corp has poured energy and resources into reproductions of ancient gray stone churches and glass skyscrapers and—all of it. All of it.

"And that's the river, modeled on the Seine River, where we'll be celebrating later," she says, pointing west.

"Celebrating what?"

"It's the day of the *Flamen Dialis*—the final day of Trinity Term. It's a very sacred day for Excelsior College and, of course, alumni. Lots of fun."

We keep driving and I try to take it all in: the stone buildings, the beautiful lawns, the happy and beautiful young people smiling and laughing in the sunshine. None of them are wearing masks. I roll down the window: the air is pure. Then we drive through the stone gates of the Scholars Club.

"Remember, your name is Lara," the surgeon says, as she parks.

We step out of the car and the surgeon strides down the bluestone path toward an ornate, redbrick building. I'm over-whelmed by everything I can see and hear and smell—I try to keep up with her but I need to stop and look.

There's a sound in the tree above me.

The surgeon turns back, irritated—then her face lights up. "Do you know what that is?"

"A . . . bird?"

"*Dacelo leachii*—a blue-winged kookaburra."

The tree it's sitting in is beautiful, with waxy red blossoms. "A flame tree," adds the surgeon. "*Brachychiton acerifolius*. The Scholars Club prides itself on its Australian collection."

•

We enter the front door of the massive Scholars Club and step into a foyer, which leads to another beautiful room with a long, wooden table, where a young woman is sitting calmly at her laptop, which seems to float above the table.

"Hi," calls the young woman, looking up.

She introduces herself as Jasmine Anderson. She's been waiting for us. She looks about a year older than I am, and she's wearing jeans and a T-shirt. I feel overdressed in my stupid red velvet dress with ruby trim. Jasmine's smooth, blond hair is tied up with a kind of cord-thing at the back. She is so gorgeous; she really is. I feel funny about being close to her, because she's a college girl and a completely different species from me.

"I understand you went to school here too, Professor Keel-ing, so I'll leave you alone to look around," Jasmine says, and the surgeon beams at her. "Just let me know if you need anything."

Jasmine starts typing away on her keyboard, but I can feel her watching me at the same time, as though I'm some sort of rare creature in whom she's taking a scientific interest. I look at the surgeon anxiously—it must be clear to Jasmine that I'm a Breeder. The surgeon smiles and squeezes my arm, hard, reminding me to act normally, and starts to show me around the room. The Scholars Club is where the surgeon lived, when she went to Excelsior. This is the library and the reading room where she studied. There are residential halls upstairs.

I'm entranced by all the lovely stuff in the room: even the pens gathered in a bunch on a desk are each uniquely beautiful. There's a massive painting down one wall of the room which the surgeon tells me is from the eighteenth century. The painting depicts a small group of people examining a strange animal on a slab, and one of the figures is pointing to it. The animal looks like bits of other animals that I've seen in pictures: part duck, part rat, or something. The title is *The Platypus*. They also have a giant fireplace. Alongside these old-fashioned pieces is all the state-of-the-art technology you might dream up. Part of me is thinking about how this wealth is built on the backs of the Breeders and all Westies. The other part of me wants to slowly lick the long line of leather-bound books.

The surgeon sees me coveting the books. "Did you know," she says, pointing to a screen at the center of the bookshelf, "that there's a center hundreds of feet beneath us that preserves the genes of all the creatures on earth? Scientists are being sent out into the badlands to retrieve genetic samples so they can be reanimated. The Scholars Club is particularly interested in the antipodean animals." She turns to me. "That screen there gives you direct access to the specimens, so you can study them. Isn't that beautiful?"

I nod. Rich people are reanimating kangaroos, while thirteen-year-old girls have rich people's babies in the Incubator. Isn't that just beautiful?

"Jasmine wants to be a scientist," the surgeon adds.

It's like Jasmine can feel me silently judging her because she looks up and narrows her eyes at me, and I feel a mad cut of hate, or wretched jealousy, or something. Jasmine is deadly bright as well as deadly hot, and she wants to be a scientist one day. I'm sure she will be. There's no danger of the Incubator for her—Jasmine is pure Corporation. She'll never be shoved somewhere and shot full of chemicals, injected and tested until she can't stand up. If she's fertile, she *will* have to suffer the Egg Retrievals just like me, though. And just like the surgeon had to. I feel a bite of mean satisfaction.

Jasmine and the surgeon look at each other, and Jasmine says, "I know you'll be living off-campus, but you'll use the library and the reading room here. And the kitchen. Come and see and have a snack."

We go into the kitchen and Jasmine opens the fridge and starts to throw stuff on the center island, which is a luscious slab of green stone, probably pilfered from a rare sacred site somewhere in the badlands.

"I'm starving," Jasmine says, chucking different types of posh cheese, dips, and fruit on the slab, making a little pyramid of food. She looks at me, her eyes laughing. I smile at her.

"Dig in," she says, shoving a cracker piled with something white into her mouth. She sighs, rolling her eyes. "That is fucking lovely. Have some of the blue cheese."

The surgeon nods at me, and I sit on a stool at the other end of the island.

"Here," she says, and smears some cheese on with a knife and holds out the cracker. I hesitate and then my stomach growls—I'm hungry too—and so reach over and take it.

Damn. She's right—it *is* fucking lovely.

After our snack, the surgeon takes me on a tour of the rest of the Scholars Club, including the residential halls on the upper floors. I meet more boys and girls who attend the college— so many that they all blend into one. They're all versions of Jasmine—impeccably dressed, clear-skinned, and polite, with unreadable expressions.

Then the surgeon wants to meet with some of her old college friends, so I spend the rest of the day walking around the grounds by myself. It's a beautiful day and at first, I'm overwhelmed by everything I see. But as the day goes on, I feel tired and melancholy—and like a total outsider.

At sunset, we meet down at the Seine.

There's a crowd of a few hundred people lining the banks: college kids, their proud parents and grandparents; alumni across many generations. Everyone is well-dressed and well-fed. No doubt they all have a staff to style their hair, do their makeup. "The most elite people are here," the surgeon whispers to me. It's the most animated I've ever seen her. I get it—they're the special ones. The most elite of the original Corporation families. And the super-producers who keep their line going. There's nothing more they love than being with each other, noticing each other, being noticed by each other.

I feel so much despair. Westies will always be kept outside the glory of this world. As for the future—it's all about making Corp kids. And then, I realize, I just made my decision: I'm going to strap explosives around my body alongside Alex and kill myself with the Response. Even though I know it will change nothing, at least I'll be standing side-by-side with Alex. And with Westies. I'm not part of the Corp; I grew up Westie, after all.

"Will?" the surgeon says.

I look over. "Sorry?"

"Come here and look!" she says. Beautiful paper lanterns are being lit and released onto the river, while uniformed staff with tiny lights in their hair bring platters of food to us down at the riverbank.

We see the dean across the crowd, seated alongside his distinguished guests in a ribboned-off VIP area. He gives us a wave and a wink. The surgeon smiles back, her eyes flat. Then she leans in and whispers to me. "He called me to say he was *uncomfortable* with our deal. Can you believe his cheek? I'm sure you're not the only unconventional enrollment here." She points to the student body. "He wants an additional ten thousand units per live birth."

I nod. Presumably she's not absorbing the loss. The surgeon keeps waving at the dean until he turns away, and then her smile disappears.

"Anyway. It's all for the best. We've decided to cut Luke out and split his units between us. I'm just letting you know so you're not shocked when things change. Luke will handle your initial enrollment and processing into the college. But after that, you won't see him: we're going to deal with potential parents directly. Luke won't find out for a few months, and by then, it will be too late."

Luke would have arranged to pay the Gray Corps a

percentage of those birth payments, and I don't think it's wise for her to cut out the Gray Corps. But I don't say anything.

•

On the journey home, the surgeon says. "You know, you could have a great life, Will. Later on, you can be a scientist and have a wife and child, just like the two women who have your baby." *Your baby*. I shudder. Everything about . . . that . . . has gone into the black box in my mind.

"The contract will be executed in two days," she continues. "You'll be locked into the Incubator overnight and then tomorrow you'll go to the college again to start your enrollment process. I can't emphasize how valuable you are."

Well. That's a comfort—or would be, if I valued my life at all.

The car pulls up at the surgeon's place. I go to open my passenger door, when the surgeon activates the central locking system. My door won't budge. She turns to me.

"I've thought about your request regarding Alex and we will go ahead with that. But I want one more egg extraction to cover my risks and expenses. So that would bring the total to five additional egg retrievals per year—all to go to me. You would still have one cycle off to recover."

I nod. "Okay."

"So we have a deal?"

I shrug. "Yes."

She looks surprised. "I thought you'd be more . . ."

"Grateful?"

"Just . . . happy." She shakes her head.

I make my mind go blank. I can't even think about the deal,

about that chance of a life with Alex—it will break me. If there were any way I could convince Alex, I would. But I can't.

The surgeon unlocks my door, and gestures to Luke to come over. "Luke will be taking you to the college tomorrow to go through your enrollment papers. I have work to do."

•

We enter the Incubator and as we walk past the cells, and past the guard stations, I can feel the rising tension—the Incubator is louder than usual. There's the sound of scuffles and raised voices, the sense that things aren't quite right. The Night of Fires is coming. Luke can feel the tension too.

We're only in my cell about half an hour when the same orange Shadow suit from the night before appears.

"We need another medical check," she says to Luke, dead-pan, and starts to process me.

Luke frowns but then he nods, and I'm taken out of my cell and down the fire exit, the Shadow yanking at my wrist. "Hurry. *Hurry*," she says.

When we reach the bottom, Cate comes around the corner, and the Shadow moves a few feet away. I step toward Cate and before she can say anything to me, I tell her, "I'll do it. Send me in with Alex."

Cate laughs. She looks furious. "Terms have changed, *Breeder runner*."

I shiver. "I'll do whatever you want. I'll give my life for the Response. I mean it."

She shakes her head. "You know, Will—there are things worse than death."

My heart leaps. "Yeah. I know that."

"Whenever the Response blows things up, do you know what the Corp does?"

"Yes," I say, remembering the court and the magistrate, and wondering where Cate is heading with this. "You're all caught and sentenced to death in the Rator."

Cate nods. "Ringleaders and Shadows are sent to the Rator. But do you know what happens to the other Responders who are still of breeding age?"

"No."

"The Corp doesn't like to waste their valuable breeding equipment. So they're strapped to beds and left to breed under sedation for a few years, until their brains are too messed-up to revolt. We call them *Bodies*. Do you understand?"

"Why are you telling me this?"

I can see that Cate is trying to calm herself. She's trying not to shout at me. "I had a little chat with Alex. She says you've got a deal with the Corp to get you both out of here."

I'm stunned. I can't believe Alex would tell Cate.

"I also hear from my sources that you're going to be a college girl," Cate says.

I don't respond.

"You're not a real Westie, are you?"

I hesitate, then shake my head.

"You're actually Corp."

She's worked it out. "Fucking hell," Cate says. She looks like she wants to murder me. I can see her restraining herself. "Okay," she says. "I planned for Alex to carry one of the first bombs on the Night of Fires. But I'm going to use her as support crew instead. Which means her future will almost certainly be as a Body."

"No. No!"

"Unless you can convince me otherwise. Do I have your attention?"

I nod.

"Good," Cate says. "Are you going to the surgeon's place again tomorrow?"

"No. To the college."

"This is what I'm going to get you to do . . . You're going to take more bomb components to the Scholars Club tomorrow. But this time, you're going to assemble them. We're going to detonate their precious collections and their precious college kids at the same time that we blow up the Incubator."

"You want me to *build* bombs? I've smuggled components, sure, but I've never built . . ."

"That's a *you* problem." Cate says.

What if I fuck it up? What happens to Alex then?

"What if . . . what if we worked together?" I say quickly. "I could be in college working for the Response. Your person on the inside. We could use their technology. Their resources. I could smuggle it all out for you. Whatever you want. For years! It seems like such a waste to just blow it all up . . ."

Cate spits on the floor. "*We*? I'm not working with you, Corp vampire." She hates me so much.

"Cate," I plead. "I understand where you're coming from. I really do. I'm angry too. But the Corp will just shut you down. Even if you blew up the whole Incubator, they'd just build another, and put more Breeders in it. There are millions outside the Wall, waiting."

Then she hits me. Right across the face—and it hurts like hell. "You'll put bombs in the college—where I tell you—and then I'll decide what happens to Alex."

I maintain eye contact with her; I don't let my hand fly up to cradle my stinging face.

"How will you . . . know the bombs have gone off?"

"Oh, we'll know, alright. You'll program the bombs to go off at 2:30 a.m., and the Night of Fires will start shortly after. If your bombs don't go off, Alex becomes a Body. If you do what we say, we'll let Alex be a suicide. Do you understand?"

"I—yes."

She smiles.

I try to calm the panic inside.

One phone call to the surgeon, tipping her off that Cate is leader of the Response, and Cate will be tortured for information and then eliminated. But where would that leave Alex? Anyone associated with Cate would be sent to the Rator, or spend the next few years as a Body.

As though Cate can read my mind, she says, "I've let my core people know the deal: if anything happens to me, even if I die tomorrow night, those bombs still better go off or Alex becomes a Body."

I nod.

"The guy in your cell is one of the surgeon's?"

"Yes."

"We'll leave him while he's needed. Then we'll take him out too. So we have a deal?"

I nod again, and she hands me three egg-shaped bombs, some tape pieces, and elastic, and watches as I work quickly to pull the bombs apart, putting their components inside my pockets and underwear.

"You'd better deliver," she says, turning away.

The orange Shadow takes me back to my cell. Luke raises his

eyebrows and I walk past him, curl onto my hard bed. I spend the night trying to think what to do.

•

The next morning, I watch Luke's face in the rearview mirror from the moment we pull out of the parking lot of the Incubator. I can feel the bomb parts pressing against my skin. I take in Luke's tired eyes, his beat-up car, the way his shoulders curl forward. It will be years and years before Luke's life will be anything like Rob's. I bet he's hoping that this deal will get him on the fast track. But the surgeon and the dean have sold him out. What if I could somehow cut another deal for him, work an angle that way? He may not want to deal with a Breeder, though—or believe me when I tell him they're cheating on him. In his mind, this deal is going ahead, and he's being paid well. After a few minutes, my heart pounding, I decide to risk it. I say, "Have you ever done a Breeder run?"

He meets my gaze in the rearview mirror. I *think* I feel the car slow a little. Then his eyes go back to the road and the car speeds up. We ride in silence for another five minutes or so.

His eyes appear in the rearview mirror again. "What do you want?" he says.

"It seems to me you could do better in this deal. I mean, speaking Westie to Westie—it's always the Corp screwing everyone over."

"You're a Breeder. What do you know? And there's no Westie alliance here—you're one of them."

"Well, I know they've done a deal behind your back."

"What do you mean?"

"You're getting your upfront payment of one hundred thousand units and then they're cutting you out completely. They're splitting the payments that come after that—for the live births—between themselves. The surgeon reckons she can do everything the Gray Corps affiliate usually does herself, through the Incubator."

"Prove they're cheating me," he says.

"I can prove it but we'd need to get someone else involved," I tell him, and he doesn't answer, so I continue. "I've thought about the way forward and my take is—the surgeon is no longer needed. We need the dean to deal with the Corp buyers—they purchase eggs through his college. But what if there were a way to cut the surgeon out of this, for the Gray Corps to deal directly with the Corp buyers and the dean? For a hell of a lot more units?"

He shakes his head. "We'd need the surgeon to shepherd through the live births or the deal wouldn't work."

"The Gray Corps would make sure she took care of those births. Especially after she tried to cheat them."

He sighs. "I don't know . . ."

"*I* know the Gray Corps," I say. "I was a Breeder runner. I worked with Robert Hunter. He's Tier 1 in the Gray Corps." I don't say, *Assuming Rob made it through and wasn't sent to the Rator*. Then again, I got to know Rob over those months at the Wall, and I bet that if anyone had a plan B, it would be Rob. He probably had to pay a lot of people off, but I also bet he had bags of units, gold bullion, pirate booty, whatever, hidden somewhere for just that reason.

I watch Rob's name register on Luke's face. My gut read on Luke was right, he's low down in the ranks.

"Do you know him?" I ask.

"*Of* him," he admits. I breathe a sigh of relief—Rob is still around.

"Someone like Rob would have the clout to cut the surgeon out and then you and Rob could split *her* fee. You'd just have to pay an incentive to the dean. Or threaten him for trying to screw over the Gray Corps. And more important than that, you'd have a basis to work with Rob in the future." He looks surprised that I know how Gray Corps hierarchy works. The catch is that I need to get Alex out too. I need the Gray Corps to arrange that. But that's not for Luke.

"And, as you know—the surgeon won't be able to touch you once the upper-tier Gray Corps is involved," I say.

I'm winging it here. My heart is pounding. His silence is unnerving me.

"I can't call Rob on my phone," I say. "But if you're interested . . . I . . . I could use your phone."

I sit back in my seat. There's nothing else to say.

Luke is quiet for the rest of the drive. He could use this deal to break into the upper tiers of the Gray Corps, but he would also be risking being sent to the Rator if the deal falls through.

When we reach the Scholars Club, he says, "What's Rob's number? I could call him on your behalf."

Does he really think I'm that stupid?

"No," I say, my heart pounding. "I need to talk to him directly."

"Fine. I'll think about it."

Luke walks me up to the stone steps of the Scholars Club, and I ring the bell. Before I say goodbye to him, I look him in the eyes, and I can see that I have his attention.

•

Jasmine answers and shows me inside. Her face is closed, wearing that mask that Corp people are so good at putting on and taking off.

"I'm working on a special project," she says, as I follow her into the library. There's a boy there too, working on a laptop.

"This is Clancy," Jasmine says. Clancy waves without looking up.

"New girl," Jasmine says to Clancy. "Niece of Professor Keeling."

Now Clancy looks up. "What's your major?"

I try my best not to stammer. "Science. Genetics, some day. I hope."

"I'm working on a genetic selection project at the moment," Clancy says. "You can have a look if you want." I go around and have a look at his computer, and he shows me some modeling. "This is for the echidna—I'm trying to edit out some of its disease-prone genes. When the modeling's finished, I'm going to try it on samples. Ultimately, we want to reanimate it—I'm hoping to be on Professor Williams's team," he says. We spend a few minutes tracing the model.

From when I was tiny, I'd stand on the Wall and watch the exploration machines. I imagined that they were discovering things to improve our lives—Westie lives, not just Corp lives. Life here doesn't have to be just about the Corp. We could work toward something else, rather than allowing the Corp to gobble up all our resources. If the Response can infiltrate the surgeon's house, why not the Scholars Club and the whole college? I can imagine a world where we could do right by Ma's legacy, through research that would mean the fertility crisis would be over, the fight for nourishment would be over, and we'd be able to reanimate the broken land, heal the blighted waterways. There wouldn't be a need for the Wall, because there'd be plenty for everyone. Why not?

I realize that Jasmine is looking right at me with that mask-face and for a split moment, I see that behind it, there's another feeling—but I can't tell what it is.

"You know, I'd better tell the tutor you're here," Jasmine says. She goes out the door and returns a couple minutes later with a woman in her twenties, who smiles and places a shiny laptop in front of me.

"Lara, isn't it?" she says. "Welcome. I'm Dr. Ellis. The dean said you'd be here today. This laptop is for you. I also have quite a few online forms for you, I'm afraid, so make yourself comfortable."

Dr. Ellis sets me up at the other end of the same large wooden table where Clancy and Jasmine are working. She pulls over a lamp with a green light. I can feel the bomb materials pressing against my skin.

"From Astor College, right?" Dr. Ellis asks. Jasmine and Clancy look up and giggle. "Ignore them," she adds. "The website's pretty self-explanatory, but I'll be in the next room if you have any questions. The others will help you if want coffee or a snack."

Her heels click away as she leaves the room.

I look at the computer screen. I've never had my own computer before—the computer I used at school was over ten years old and leased from the Corp at a cost of five units per week. Clancy and Jasmine go back to work as I start answering the questions on the forms. I type in my answers, enjoying the fictional life of Lara Goode, but my mind is racing. I have to find a place and time to plant the bombs. I have to work out *how* to set up the bombs. What I want most, of course, is to make a deal with the Gray Corps and get Alex out altogether, but what if Luke isn't a risk-taker, or worse, what if Rob won't take my call? In that case, unless I succeed with the bombs, Alex suffers a worse fate than death. I touch the outline of the bomb components under my dress.

"Lara?" Jasmine is smirking at me.

It takes me a moment to realize that Jasmine is speaking to me. "Sorry. What?"

"I said, do you know Clarice Euston?"

"Who?"

She smirks again. "She goes to Astor. She would've been in your year."

"Oh. Probably. I . . . I tended to keep to myself." I feel my face go hot. "Why is Astor funny to you?"

"No reason," she says, and smiles. "It's just that Astor's known as a big party school, is all. And you, uh, don't seem like the type." She shrugs. "By the way, *where* did you get that dress? I *love* it."

Is this what I can expect over the next four years? I need a cigarette. I don't say anything to Jasmine or Clancy, who don't look up as I walk past. I sit on the stoop of the Scholars Club and light up, staring at the Latin motto carved into the ground.

Sitting outside in the fresh air, I watch the college boys and girls walk across the lawns, laughing, talking, happy. I think about Ma. All that work she did for the Corp—so many days, weeks, *years* of terrible labor. All the children she had for them. All her psychological and physical pain. Would Ma blow up the Scholars Club, their collections and their college kids, all tucked up in their residential halls? All those kids with dreams of their own? I feel the answer in my gut: Ma would do everything, anything, for the person she loved.

I go back inside and work on the forms again. Then, when Jasmine and Clancy are absorbed in their work, I go to the bathroom and lock myself in a stall and take all the bomb components out. My hands shaking, I line them up on top of the cistern—three bombs, three sets of ten components. I'm so anxious I could be sick, because I've never built a bomb before, but I know how things work—at the plant, I was often working with new machines, and my hands just seemed to know what to do. I pick up the first set of components, one by one, and get them to interlock easily. The hardest part to place is the timer: a little battery-powered pack with wires. It takes me a number of goes but finally I work out how it fits with the other parts. Then I hear the bathroom door open.

"Lara?" It's Jasmine. She's outside my stall.

"Yeah?" My throat is hoarse. I clear my throat and try again. "Yes?"

"Are you okay?"

"Sure. Just . . . ah, you know. Stomach issues."

"Oh. Okay." I can almost hear what she's thinking in response: *how abject*.

I wait to hear the outside door close, and then I flick the switch to activate the timer so I can program it.

Nothing happens. I turn the device around and around in my hand, trying to work out the problem. Then I take it apart and try assembling the bomb all over again. Still not working. I put it aside and assemble the second and third units. Their timers won't work either, the electronics just aren't animating. I take the lid off the cistern, take out a wire from the top of the toilet mechanism, and use it to open the back of the first battery pack. It's empty. I open the second and third. They're all empty. I feel a chill from my toes to my head. Cate. Cate took the batteries out. I'm sure of it. She wants my bombing mission to fail so that she can tell the Responders that Alex has to become a Body. So

I'll spend the rest of my days living with the guilt of that, know- ing it's my fault. She hates me that much.

There's a firm knock on the stall door. "Lara? It's Dr. Ellis. Jasmine said you've been in here half an hour." Her tone is angry, rather than concerned. Fuck.

"Yes, Doctor. Just feeling a little sick. I'll be right out."

"I need you out here right now," she says, firmly.

I sweep the components into the tampon disposal unit. Then I flush the toilet, open the stall door to see Dr. Ellis's stern face, and follow her out.

My only hope of protecting Alex is the possibility of Luke deciding to take up my offer, and then Rob helping me out the rest of the way. Which, to be honest, doesn't feel like much hope at all.

•

I get into the back of Luke's car. The air is icy. Luke says nothing.

We drive for ten minutes and then Luke suddenly pulls the car over and hands me his phone.

"Call Rob on video," he says. He watches me type in Rob's number—after all these months, I still know it by heart. Then we wait.

A video call opens up.

"*Will?*" It's Rob. He now looks middle-aged. He's thin and balding and there are wrinkles in his neck but he's dressed well, in a beautiful linen suit. He shows no reaction to my transformed appearance. He's not a good guy, but I'm so relieved to see him.

I know I have to work quickly. "Yeah, it's me. I'm here with Luke Stone, a Tier—" Luke holds up six of his fingers. "Tier 6 Gray Corps affiliate. I've . . . I've been in the Incubator and now I'm part of a contract between the dean of Excelsior, the chief surgeon who runs the Incubator, and the Gray Corps," I tell him. "I'm genetically Corp and am a super-producer," I say, my face burning. I explain the rest of my history to him and the deal I want between the Gray Corps and the dean. "If you're brought in, we could cut the surgeon out, and you could arrange better terms for the Gray Corps. You and Luke could have the surgeon's cut, less a sweetener to the dean."

"I'm listening," he says. "What are the total numbers?"

"It was one hundred thousand units upfront and then twenty thousand each per live birth, estimated at two hundred forty per year. That's almost five million a year each. But the dean and surgeon cut another deal—they cut out Luke and the Gray Corps altogether. Say they'll handle the laundering of the babies into the Corp themselves. We would need to give the dean a much better total. He already knows the Gray Corps is involved."

Rob shows no reaction. "What's your side of it?"

"The surgeon promised me a Zone B profesh life, a house, with an initial payment of ten thousand units, out of her cut, then fifty thousand at the end of the contract. I want at least that in the new deal."

"And the dean's loyalty to the surgeon?"

"They seem friendly, but I couldn't sense any long-standing personal connection. So long as he's not exposed, of course."

"Of course. And Luke?"

Luke stiffens. I smile at him. "Luke's solid."

"I'll look into this. If it's the case that they've undersold the Gray Corps, they'll need to be punished. We'll cut out the surgeon, of course. We'll deal with the dean. Luke and I will split the Gray Corps's share," Rob says, and I give Luke the thumbs up. "And if all goes well, there may be future deals," Rob adds.

I see the greed in Luke's eyes.

"Do you want me to approach another college to see if I can raise the purchase price?"

"No," I say, thinking of the genetic collection in the Scholars Club. "I want Excelsior." I need to raise the question of Alex. I take a breath. "I also need you to run someone out of the Incubator. Can you do that?"

He hesitates. "Probably," he says. "For a price."

Luke's expression changes. He looks angry because I didn't mention this. I press on.

"We'll need contact with the Response to get her out."

Now Luke looks at me in alarm.

"Okay," Rob says, unfazed as ever. "That would be between you and me. First I need to do some background checks."

"We don't have long." I look at Luke. Any remaining loyalty he has to the surgeon is about to be cut by Rob's call, so I press ahead. "My girlfriend has to be taken out before midnight tonight. The Response is planning an attack." Luke's face goes blank.

"I'll be in touch soon," Rob says.

"Just a minute," Luke says, and he signals for me to get out of the car so he can talk to Rob himself. I hesitate, wondering if he's going to sell me out and negotiate his own contract with Rob. But it's out of my hands at this point. I've done all I can do. As I close the door, I can hear Rob soothing him, using his best negotiator voice.

•

Luke gets out of the car and starts smoking a cigarette—offering me the pack. We stand there waiting, leaning against the car doors.

"Thanks for vouching for me with Rob," he says.

I'm surprised. It's just business. "No problem," I say.

"Were you really a Breeder runner?" he asks.

"Yeah."

"So you were a Crystal boy?"

"Yeah. You were a Breeder runner too?"

He nods. "For a long time I was. I moved into logistics a couple of years ago. It's not as lucrative, but I wanted to get ahead."

Logistics means general, low-level, shit-kicking Gray Corps stuff.

"So this deal with the surgeon—it's your first time out on your own?"

"My uncle works as a driver for the surgeon—and, knowing his family ties to the Gray Corps, she asked if he knew of anyone who might help broker the deal. Just luck, really."

I nod.

We've gone through about four cigs each by the time Rob calls back.

"Everything you said checks out," he says. "And you were right about the deal between the surgeon and the dean: they agreed to cut Luke out. I'm going to offer the dean ten thousand units, going forward."

"And the surgeon?"

"The surgeon gets nothing. In return, I won't tell the Gray Corps about her betrayal." Meaning—she won't get her legs hacked off on the way home from the opera. "So, Luke. That means twenty-five thousand each live birth for you and me," he says. "With the dean to contact us for future deals. And Luke—the surgeon's one hundred thousand sign-up fee will go to you."

Luke nods. I can see his face light up beneath the cool exterior.

"We need to talk terms for your Breeder run, Will," Rob says to me.

"In exchange for me bringing this deal to you, I want you to run a person—Alex Winterson—from the Incubator to the Gray Zone," I tell him, "and I want half of my initial ten thousand units to be given to Alex; the other half held for me, for after my college term."

"Will, I won't see those egg retrieval units for a year. For a rescue and contact with Responders in the Gray Zone—I need an extra five thousand units upfront. There will be still be five thousand units for Alex, if you want, or you could have two thousand five hundred each. And the Gray Corps will honor the fifty thousand unit payment the surgeon promised you, and the house in Zone B, but that's not until the end of your contract."

"Give it all to Alex." *Fuck.* He and Luke are making so much off me, it kills me that my upfront amounts are so small. But fuck it.

"I'll lock it all in and then send people to get Alex out tonight."

•

When we get back to the Incubator, security checks our IDs thoroughly, and for the first time they give us not only a pat-down, but make us go through the screens. As we go up to my cell, everything is dead quiet. Eerily quiet.

When we reach my cell, we sit down without saying a word. Luke breaks the silence.

"Do you know how to use these?" Luke asks, pointing to the Taser and a semiautomatic clipped into his belt.

"No."

He takes them out one at a time and shows me—in case something goes wrong.

"When it's time—when Rob's people arrive, or the Night of Fires starts, whichever happens first—I'll give you the Taser. Okay?"

"Thanks."

"And if anything happens to me—take my gun."

"Okay. What time is it?"

"It's just after nine p.m."

The next three hours are going to feel like the longest in history.

•

Midnight comes and goes, but there's no sign from Rob.

One a.m. comes and goes, and there's still no sign.

Two a.m. comes and goes, and nothing. Luke and I are quiet, keeping ourselves calm but I'm sure we're thinking the same thing: What if Rob made a deal with the dean and is fucking off with everyone's units? I mean, he'll still need to come and get me out, but both Luke and Alex are disposable.

Then: the walls are shaking. The sprinklers open and cold water is pouring down on me. The sliding doors open and two orange suits come in.

"Out! Out! Out!" they scream at me. I can tell they're afraid, which makes me afraid too.

I'm stunned, and Luke drags me into the corridor. Outside my cell is absolute chaos—orange suits shooting each other with their pistols and Tasers, and beating each other with their batons, and I can't tell which orange suits are the Responders, and which are Corp. Around the southern curve of the Circle, the Breeders, bellies different sizes, are lined up, interspersed by more orange suits. They're being led outside—by the Responders? The Corp? I can't tell and I can't see anyone's faces.

Then there's a deep blast that feels like it's coming through the walls, and everyone screams. I am thrown against a wall and when I stand up, I see fire roaring down the Circle corridor opposite me. The electronics in the security system must have failed because all the sliding doors are shuddering open. When the lights go out, the screaming gets louder.

"Change of plan," Luke says, and takes the semiautomatic from his belt and gives it to me, leaving him with just the Taser. I put the gun under the elastic still wrapped around my body.

Two orange suits herd the Breeders from my corridor to the fire escape. Luke is next to me, pushing me down the hall. I don't know where the rest of the orange suits are running. I look into the faces of the Breeders in the crowd. I haven't seen any of them before.

"What time is it?" I ask the Breeder next to me.

"It must be two thirty," she says.

"Do you know what's happened?"

"The east wing of the Incubator was bombed," she says. She makes a sign across her lips, and then across her heart. She looks scared and defiant. "There were twenty-four Breeder deaths already. Goodspeed to them all."

Out of the smoke emerge two orange Shadow suits—Responders—heading toward me. Luke sees them too, and he reaches for his Taser, but one of them hits him in the head with her baton and he crumples to the floor. Before I can grab my pistol, I'm taken out of the line and shoved down the corridor, ahead of the others. I hear more blasts and I'm shoved along the corridor and down the fire escape into the bright night, where amongst the chaos and the spot fires, Cate is standing with three orange suits. One of them is Alex.

Alex turns away from me.

Cate nods and the three of them get to work, placing devices around me.

"No bombs went off, Will," she says. "You know what that means." I look at Alex, who won't meet my eye. She's fixing a device to my arm while Cate points a semiautomatic at me.

Then Cate opens her phone.

"What's the surgeon's number?" she asks me. I look at Alex, hesitate, and then tell Cate.

Then I see the surgeon's face on video.

"Hi!" Cate beams at the surgeon.

"Where's Will?"

"Look who I've got here!" She points the camera at me.

"Will? Don't worry—security's on its way."

"Right, but will they make it before your precious Corp princess explodes?" Cate asks. "Tell you what. I'll keep her alive if you open the gates of the Incubator immediately."

We all look instinctively at the huge iron gates that are two hundred feet away.

From where I'm standing, I can see the surgeon's face flicker. She's not going to risk her life for a Breeder.

Cate smiles. "In that case, I'll let you watch!" she says, and laughs. The orange suits finish attaching the wires onto me. Alex approaches Cate with a little device—the detonator.

Then Alex meets my gaze, I see something cross her face, and she turns and runs, holding the detonator out to her side.

Cate raises the semiautomatic and aims it at Alex. I throw my entire weight at Cate, knocking us both to the ground.

Cate is shooting at the air, trying to shoot me. I manage to land a solid punch in her stomach and another to her face, sending blood pouring out of her nose. I get up and run. I can hear Cate getting to her feet, stumbling, and then I hear the bullets fly out—she's firing at me, at us. I'm running toward Alex, zig-zagging. An orange suit appears out of nowhere and Tasers me in the back, at my shoulder. I tumble to the ground from the impact; see the orange suits approach. I get up, take the pistol out from beneath my tracksuit, and start shooting. I've never shot a gun before. I see a bloom of blood on the thigh of the first suit. Then Cate is in front of me; I close my eyes and fire, and Cate groans and falls. I've shot her in the heart. I get up, and I keep running, until I reach the fire escape. Alex is waiting for me.

•

I follow Alex back up the fire-exit stairs, then past rows and rows of empty cells. I keep shouting her name, but in the roar of voices and the flames, it's hopeless. Then I see her stop. Small and wiry, she stares right into me, and her face screws up. She looks like she might cry.

"Alex!"

She comes forward as if to hug me, hesitates, and steps back. The detonator is still in her hand.

"Alex—come with me! I can take you to the Gray Zone tonight."

She looks at me, and it's as though she's come back.

"We can do it, Alex. You deserve to have a life."

I can see that in this moment, she wants to do it, and I can imagine it all: getting her back to the Gray Zone, being in contact with her while I'm at the college. And then eventually, both of us living together in Zone B.

Then her eyes change.

She takes my hand, points at the bombs on me and holds up the detonator. "No Zone B life, Will. Come on. Hold me. Let's just do this."

"No. Alex. Dying like this won't achieve anything. Please, let's . . ."

"Fuck off, then!" she shouts at me. I grab her and we struggle. She elbows me in the jaw. She's still got the detonator and I've still got all the explosives strapped to me. I flick the detonator out of her hand and wrestle her onto the ground.

"Fuck off, Will! I just want to . . ."

"I know."

"So let me!"

"No."

"I hate you."

"That's okay, you can hate me."

She punches me, hard, in the face. I pull myself over and kick the detonator farther out of reach. She goes to punch me again, and I block her, try to kick her, miss. Then an orange suit is standing in the corridor with us and I see that it's Luke. Luke grabs Alex around the waist. She screams at him. He pulls her arms around her back and pins them there. "Will!" he says. "Reach into my back pocket—I've got some ties in there." I get the hand ties and, my hands shaking, I secure them around Alex's wrists, while Alex yells how much she hates me. Then Luke throws Alex over his shoulder and we run. We carry her down the fire escape, across the parking lot, and to Rob's SUV, where he's waiting. She's still shouting at me. I gently place her inside, in the back seat, and slam the door.

"Good to go!" I shout at Rob, and smack the hood. I watch him take off.

I know that Alex may never forgive me for this. But I can live with that. I wouldn't have been able to live with myself if she took her own life, even if it was for a cause she believed in. I believe in her, and all that she can do for the Response—alive. Ma always said that betrayal can feel cruel, but there's love behind it. And maybe one day, who knows, Alex herself will understand why I did what I did.

•

In the morning, Luke is driving me back to the surgeon's house when he passes his phone to me—a message from Rob. I click on the link and there's the video, time-stamped a few hours ago. It's a feed of Alex walking to an apartment door, knocking. Then the door opens and her mom, sick and thin, shouts in delight and hugs her. She's back in the Gray Zone. She's safe.

My eyes tear up and I look out the window as we zip past the apartment buildings at the edge of Zone A. People are already out, walking with coffee in their hands.

When we arrive at the surgeon's house, the surgeon runs outside, pulls me out of the car and gives me a big, fake hug, hurting my shoulder more. "I was *so* worried about you!" she gushes. "Luckily, we had the Response shut down by dawn and the ringleaders are already awaiting trial. We lost one hundred twenty-two good Breeders in the blast—not all the bodies have been identified." She leans over and whispers. "We haven't yet accounted for your girlfriend, Alex."

She shows Luke and me inside, into a small room I haven't seen before.

"It's time for *kaffee und kuchen*," she says. "You must be starved." There's a delicate tablecloth on the table, and a young man is playing Bach's *Goldberg Variations* on a piano. The surgeon shows me to my seat. From where I sit, I can see outside the gigantic windows to the street outside, where Rob's gold SUV is just pulling up to the curb.

"Well. I should hear that your deeds have been executed any minute now," the surgeon says, taking her seat across from us. "Actually, before you get comfortable—would you mind changing out of that tracksuit? It's such an eyesore."

I shake my head. "No."

"What do you mean, *no*?" she laughs, and points to a dress a member of her staff is holding. I become conscious of my body again. Once upon a time, my body was mine to do things with—to run, climb, punch, kick. Then, when I was in the Incubator, it was a thing for other people to use, and it wasn't mine at all. Now, it's something in between: this body is still being used, but at least it's a better exchange.

"I'm not wearing that dress," I say. The surgeon once said that college girls always present themselves as feminine, that it was a "marketing thing," but I'm with the Gray Corps now. I'm not wearing dresses ever again. And I'm going to shave my head, close to the skin—like all Westie males.

The surgeon sits there, staring at me. I sip my coffee and think about how I won't have the surgeon's mentoring after this deal. Instead, I'll have an enemy for life. But I'll have the protection of both the Corp—through the dean—and the Gray Corps. I'll live on-site at the Scholars Club and learn for myself. I'll be a weird kid—I'll never lose that.

The surgeon is about to say something else to me when there's a knock at the front door and one of the staff is beside her, talking to her in a low voice.

"No, they don't have an appointment!" the surgeon tells her staff. "No, I don't see why they're here, the deal has been done . . ."

The staff member whispers something else.

"Okay, fine. Show them in."

Moments later Rob comes in, smiling, the dean of Excelsior beside him.

The surgeon's face is a picture.

•

My name is Lara Goode. I'm majoring in science at Excelsior, the most elite college in the Corporation. I can see the ocean from my bedroom at the top of the Club's terrace, and I'm learning how to craft human DNA in the Scholar Club's laboratory. When I graduate, I'm planning to do a PhD.

I know who I really am. And I know that Alex is safe. Like all Breeders, I'm taking the long view, and biding my time.

ACKNOWLEDGMENTS

I would like to express my great appreciation for my agent, Julia Kenny, of Dunow, Carlson & Lerner Literary Agency, for her brilliant work on behalf of *Breeder*. Warmest thanks to my incredible editor, Vikki Warner. Thanks also to the wonderful Blackstone Publishing team—Kathryn G. English, Mandy Earles, Megan Wahrenbrock, and Samantha Benson—and to Corinna Barsan for her transformative editorial insights.